The Influencer Witch

Date With a Vampire

T.D. Magnus

Table of Contents

Prologue

Before I could scream out for Joe to stop, he grabbed the locket on my chest—the one that had been passed down through generations of witches. The locket glowed, the light blinding and illuminating everything around us until my surroundings were no longer visible.

Our baby screamed, crying with a terror in her voice I'd never heard.

And then, Joe was gone. Nothing remained of the man I'd loved with more passion and ferocity than any other.

But I couldn't stop, couldn't grieve. He'd sacrificed his entire being to give me the strength to get out of the cave with our child. I couldn't tarnish his memory by falling apart now.

Seizing the locket in my palm, I channeled his magical energy, using every bit of force I had to collapse the cave. Rocks crumbled to the ground, building over top of one another until they trapped that damned being in its place.

But it was still alive, and we needed to run.

With Isabel in my arms, I ran as fast as my feet would push me, replaying everything that had happened.

Joe had tried to warn me. He had tried to tell me we weren't strong enough to go up against that creature, but I wouldn't listen—I was too worried about getting our baby back. I'd jerked my arm from his grasp, ignoring his repetitive warnings. I knew where I stood, and I wasn't backing down.

So foolish! So naive.

Yes, my powers had shrunk with my reluctance to embrace the role of town witch, but I knew I was far stronger than he gave me credit for— a vampire would be nothing to defeat. I could do it with my eyes closed.

Slowly, we'd crept to the cave's edge, to the lair of the vampire who'd stolen my child in retribution. Inside the cave was old and tattered furniture, set up like an ordinary living room.

Without so much as a word, I'd summoned my magic, lifting the couch silently as I crashed it into the creature that stood shrouded in shadows.

The memory sent a shiver through me, and I gripped Isabel tighter as I ran. *Why did I have to be so stupid?*

He had known we were there. I'd charged into the cave, grabbing every piece of furniture my magic would carry, screaming for my husband to get our baby back while I distracted our enemy.

But the monster's movements had been too quick, evading everything I'd thrown his way. And his strength was truly unmatched, unlike any vampire I'd encountered.

The hardest part was when the realization began to settle in. *Joe was right. He's too powerful for me to defeat. We'll never make it out alive.*

I had turned and ran, hoping to steer him away from my family. But Joe had stood at the entrance of the cave with Isabel, not leaving like I'd begged him to.

Handing over our daughter, he looked at me resolutely. I held Isabel in my arms protectively as I tried to stop him, to beg him not to do what I knew he had planned. But his tone was fierce, confirming every fear I held. He choked on the words, giving Isabel a kiss on the temple before grabbing my head and pulling me closer to brush his lips against mine as he reached for the locket.

And in a flash, he was gone.

Now, with Isabel in my arms, I didn't stop running until I reached our home. When I placed Isabel in her bassinet, I realized a bright burn covered the top of her face by her temple. Where Joe had kissed her before he left. Where the locket had glowed too bright, enough to burn her skin where she was uncovered by my arms.

I kissed her burn, enchanting my lips so the kiss would heal her, and slowly rocked her to sleep.

Stepping onto the front porch, I crumpled to the ground, sobbing and grieving the loss of my husband, my love. Without him, I wasn't whole. An emptiness filled me, tormenting me with guilt.

It was my fault. I should have listened to his warning, but I didn't. Now he was gone. And when he left, he took a piece of me with him.

I allowed myself time to grieve, to feel the pain of loss and heartbreak. And once I felt I could stand, I forced myself to be strong, to push those feelings aside. Because now I was the sole parent of our children. I needed to be impervious. For them. For our girls. Joe would want it like that.

In a numb daze, I collected Rhiannon from our kind neighbor and brought her home to the house absent of her father. And then I had to deliver the devastating news to a child who was too young to understand.

And when she fell asleep, I wept some more, only allowing myself the weakness when I was alone.

For them. Everything from here on out would be for them. And when they were old enough, our coven would grow strong enough to defeat the vile creature that took my husband.

They would all pay.

Chapter 1:

Heart

It wasn't the first time I'd seen this image. Creatures. Humanlike creatures feasting on someone, devouring them like wild beasts. Blood filled the edges of my mirror, where I'd witnessed the grotesque scene more than once. Dripping down their faces, pooling beneath the poor soul they fed upon.

But the image was blurry. It was always blurry—enough to intrigue me, to scare me to my core, but never enough to get a clear visual.

I swiped the post-shower steam from the mirror, hoping to see the scene with clarity. But as usual, there was nothing. Nothing but my stupid red hair that frizzed in every direction. Nothing but my green eyes, which stood out more than I wanted them to. Nothing but the burn scar on my face, marking me for life.

Looking in the mirror, I saw *nothing*.

I shook it off, thinking once again that I was going crazy. I mean, why else would I see things that clearly weren't there? Things that would probably get me locked up in a straitjacket.

The townspeople would love that. They would love to throw my family into a padded room, locking us away from the rest of civilization. We were the weird family—the outcasts. The family with the house that sits on the edge of town because that was where we belonged. Away from others.

I used to wonder why people would call us strange. What had we done to deserve the reputation? It was always some big riddle I could never figure out. But seeing weird things in the reflections of light or water— in the mirror before school—no wonder they thought we were crazy. *I* was beginning to think so, too.

Despite the jarring vision I'd hallucinated, I grabbed my backpack and headed out the door in my typical attire: brown suede pants, a flowy green shirt, and my plain-Jane shoes. My mother said I had an earthy style, though I preferred to call it what it was—ugly.

My clothes were far from what the other girls at school would wear. And yet, no matter how much I resented them, I still wore them every day. What could I say? Those suede pants were comfortable.

Pushing past the crowd in the bustling hallways, I headed to my locker to grab my books before class. A loud call down the hall caused me to look back. When I did, I bumped into someone, knocking their books to the floor.

"Oh, I'm so sorry," I muttered, bending down to help pick them up. I handed the books to the kid in front of me. James, I think? I recognized him from one of my classes but couldn't recall a single time I'd ever heard him speak up in class. How strange that I couldn't seem to remember anything about him. Otherwise, it was as if he ceased to exist. Always forgotten in the shadows.

Though, being forgotten might be better than the hell I faced on a daily basis. The teasing and taunting. Maybe James had the right idea. Or, maybe James was lonely, an outsider who kept to himself. Someone who has trouble making friends. *I know the feeling, James.*

I had no friends. Pathetic as it was, I had to hide the "friends" button on my social media so no one would know just how much of a loser I was.

I had my sister, Rhiannon. She was my rock. And my mother, Jo. She was my safety. Might as well throw in the stray cat we've adopted, Biscuit. They're a closer friend than anyone at my school.

Do I like it? No. But how do you change it?

I smiled to James and apologized once more for bumping into him.

"Don't worry about it," he said with a smile, granting me more of a courtesy than most others here would have.

I nodded sheepishly and turned away.

What if he did have trouble making friends? Maybe I should invite him to lunch. He seemed nice enough. Maybe he could use the friend.

I turned back. "Hey, would you—" He was gone. Vanished. Disappeared among the crowd of students.

What was I doing? I suddenly had no idea why I was looking down the hall or what words I had been about to speak.

Maybe I really was going crazy…

Oh, well. I shrugged and moved on, heading to my locker. As I stood there, grabbing my books, my entire world shifted. My luck had turned had finally come to a change.

Jack—an older boy who was friends with the guys on the football team—leaned against the locker beside mine and looked at me with a crooked smile, one dimple teasing me. I would've pinched myself to make sure I wasn't dreaming, but I was already labeled as the weird girl. Didn't need that haunting me, too.

"Isabel, right?"

I nodded, unable to speak. Heck, I was unable to breathe. *Jack* was standing beside my locker, talking to me.

"Uh—yeah. That's me," I choked out a little too eagerly. I couldn't help it; this had never happened to me before, and I didn't know how to act around a cute boy.

He pointed to a poster on the wall—one with glitter letters and puffy paint, advertising the dance. "You going to the dance on Saturday?"

No? I wasn't planning on it. But was he asking me to the dance? He didn't outright say it; he only asked if I was going. Maybe he was getting a tally of everyone in school who is and isn't going, and I was getting all excited over nothing.

"I might go," I answered. A normal answer, except the way that I spoke sounded like a jumbled mess, my words both too quiet and too loud. Navigating ordinary teenage milestones was not my forte.

"Oh, yeah?" he asked, swiping his hair back and casting me a gorgeous smile.

I thought about brushing back my own hair but didn't want to draw attention to that frizzy mess, so I leaned against my locker, matching his pose. Though, his was much cooler, more sophisticated than mine. But he seemed to like the motion.

With a single nod, he said, "You should come to the dance with me."

Now I definitely had to pinch myself. There was no way this could be reality. Not my reality, anyway. But who was I to deny fate the chance to finally let me be like the other girls?

"Okay," I answered, nodding my head. "That sounds great."

He bumped the locker twice with his fist, like he was finalizing our date with the motion. "Great," he answered, standing up straight. His hand ran along my arm as he walked away, giving me a wink. "I'll see you there."

I nodded excitedly, leaning against the locker as I blew out a breath, clutching my books to my chest. My arm still buzzed from the electricity of his touch. For a brief, fleeting moment, I'd been touched by a boy. *I'd been touched by a boy!* Excitement bubbled in my chest at the possibilities. *He noticed me.* And not for my burn or my weird family, but for *me*.

Sighing blissfully, I closed my eyes, allowing myself to visualize those possibilities, to dream them.

"You don't actually think he's interested, do you?"

The voice could have been my own skepticism and fear calling out to me, but it wasn't. It was the mean girl. The queen bee. The girl who pretty much ruled the school with her well-manicured iron fist.

Rachel.

I opened my eyes to see her typical sneer staring back at me, her two minions following closely behind her. "Why would Jack be interested in you? You're a frizzy little burned girl."

Her hands swung down, knocking my tablet from my hands to the floor. The strangest sensation pulsed through me, riddling my arms with goosebumps as my tablet fell to the ground.

"Oops," she cackled, turning on her heels and walking away, pompous and with her chin held high.

Lindsay and Amanda—her two sidekicks—stood there laughing. They'd follow her lead right over the edge of a cliff if it meant they could be a part of the queen bee's hive.

I crouched down and grabbed my tablet from the floor, shoving it into my bag, cursing under my breath. Despite my hippie appearance, I was a tech whiz, which meant most of my notes were on my electronics. Past experience taught me to get an extra strong case for moments like this, ensuring my precious tablet would remain safe.

Maybe one day, I would say something to Rachel. One day. But doing so meant I'd be even more alienated from the others. Not like it could get much worse...

The bell rang and I zipped up my bag, throwing it over my shoulder. But before I stood up, I noticed a cell phone on the floor. I picked it up and flipped it around; a bubblegum pink case with colorful rhinestones covered the back. Rachel must have dropped her phone.

I stood there with the equivalent of a gold mine in the palm of my hands, debating what to do with it. Should I go through the phone? Maybe send out an embarrassing text to Jack saying she needed someone to bring her a spare pair of pants because she pooped in her other ones. Tempting. It was definitely tempting, but that would be wrong.

My mother had always told me that no matter how mean someone else was, it didn't change who *I* was. And then she would remind me that I'm a kind person. One who is selfless and treats others with decency.

Damn conscience.

Rather than doing something petty, I shoved the phone in my pocket, rushing to first period.

Coming through the door late, the teacher motioned for me to sit, and I took the seat behind Rachel. As she faced the front, I slipped the phone into the purse at her feet.

Maybe I should have done something petty with the phone, or maybe it was best that I returned it. Didn't matter. It was back now, and I had squandered the opportunity.

But it was in my nature to help others. Even when I so desperately wanted to do the opposite, it was like there was a pull on my heart that said no. My mother raised me to be kind, teasing me that it's in our blood, a family trait.

Yet, this innate desire to help people was always something I did with discretion. Was it because helping others didn't require praise, as my mother suggested? Or was I too much of a coward to face people directly, too awkward by their presence to approach them?

Either way, I blamed my kindness on my mother—something I occasionally resented her for. Though, I knew deep down that it was a good trait, even if it stung to put that phone back in Rachel's purse.

Despite her teasing, I was excited about the Homecoming dance. I had a date! An actual date! My first date ever. Honestly, it was my first interaction with a boy that was more than, "Do you have a pencil?", or "Can we borrow this chair?"

All class it was in my mind, stealing my focus from my studies. Toward the end of class, when we were allowed to talk quietly to our peers, I heard talk about the championship game that would take place at the end of the season, which we'd made every year.

Jack wasn't on the football team, but he was friends with everyone who was—teetering on the edge of popular-cool and rebel-cool, to put it simply. Though he wasn't the sexiest man on the team, as Rachel would put it, he was definitely attractive and had a lean like James Dean—cool and suave.

What would it be like to date someone like that? Someone who wasn't quite the golden boy of the school but was edgy enough to stand out and still be cool. Someone who wasn't so intimidating with his presence, but still gave me goosebumps when he was near.

If we started dating, would he invite me to one of their parties after the game? I'd never been invited to one. Though, that didn't stop me and Rhi from crashing them. Generally, we would just walk in with another group and get a few drinks as we made fun of all the normal people in school, performing their normal teenage shenanigans. It was our own ritual to make ourselves feel better about never being invited.

But since Rhi had started community college in our sleepy, suburban town of Hadley outside of Chicago, going to parties meant I'd more than likely be attending solo—and that was more might than I could conjure. Yet, it didn't stop my mind from imagining the possibilities...

***

Elated, I rushed through the front door, knowing Rhi didn't have class today. "Rhi!" I called out, dropping my bag to the floor and charging up the stairs. "You'll never believe what happened!"

Rhi's head popped out of her small, dimly lit art studio. The dingy backdrop on her wall was caked in dust and dirt—both from her art and from the age of our run-down house. As if Rachel needed more ammo to tease me over—thank god she's never seen my house.

"What's going on?" she asked with smears of clay across her forehead and cheek.

"Pfft!" I blew out a laugh, gesturing to her face before I resumed my excitement. "You will never believe what happened in school today..." I trailed off, playing a drum roll in my mind. "Jack asked me to the Homecoming dance! Isn't that crazy!"

Rhi smiled, nodding along with my excitement, but I knew her. She was wary. Something about this prohibited her from being on the same level of enthusiasm that I was.

"What? What is it? Why aren't you happy?" I asked, my insecurities taking over.

"No, it's nothing. I'm happy for you. Really." Her smile wasn't sincere. She didn't have the squinty lines around her eyes that she got when she was genuinely smiling.

"Then why do you look like you just inhaled a fart? That is not the look of excitement, Rhi. And with news like this, I expect excitement!"

"I swear, I'm excited."

"But…" I waved my hand, urging her along. *Quit beating around the bush and tell me why you're not excited.* "Rhiannon Duport, if you don't tell me this instant why you're not overflowing with glee, I swear I will shave your head when you sleep."

My threat was hollow—empty promises—and I knew she knew that. But I gave her a stern glare that demanded she tell me anyway.

"It's just… *Why?* Don't get me wrong, you are definitely worth going to Homecoming with, but it's so out of character. Why the sudden interest?"

"Jeez, thanks. Is it so hard to believe I could be asked to the dance?" My arms were crossed, and I tapped my foot waiting for a response.

"It's not that," Rhi said, rolling her eyes at my dramatic behavior. "But he never showed you the slightest of interest before. No smitten glances or even a simple hello. And now he's asking you to the dance? I just don't want you to get hurt, Isa."

"I won't. Maybe he was just too shy to talk to me before. Or maybe he just noticed me and wanted to ask me out. Is that so hard to believe?"

Rhi chewed her lip, mulling over the idea. "I guess not. And hey, if you're excited, then I'm excited." She smiled, though I could tell it was forced. But at least she was giving me some effort. Grabbing my hands, she jumped up and down, squealing like a stuck pig. "Your first date!"

Maybe she was trying a bit *too* hard to be excited, but I'd take it. I bounced with her, squealing just as loud. Why not? It was worth celebrating.

Sure, Rhi might think that I'm getting my hopes up, or being too naive about it. And maybe I knew better, that it wasn't a fairy tale come true. Still, I pushed past the doubt to enjoy my moment of happiness.

"You know what? Since it's your first date, I think this calls for something special." She reached around her neck, unclasping the necklace that draped over her chest.

The family heirloom. The special sun-shaped locket.

She placed the locket in my hand, and I turned it over, looking at it from all angles. The golden locket—still as new as the day our family got it as if it had never been worn. The gold was still vibrant with intricate and delicate designs engraved within the metal.

I was in awe.

"You're giving this to me?" I asked, breathlessly.

"I thought you might want to look good for your dance," she said with a wink. "Now turn around, let me hook it for you."

I pulled my hair up, holding it in place as Rhi's hands pulled the locket around my neck, clasping it at the back. Steering my face toward the mirror in the hallway, she said, "Look." My reflection was usually the last thing I wanted to see, but Rhi forced me, always attempting to make me feel beautiful.

But when I peered into the mirror, the locket glowed in the reflection. And within that glow, I saw red. Blood red. The same red that tainted the edges of my vision that morning.

Holy crap, I really was going crazy!

I glanced down at the locket, and there was no blood or glowing. Only the golden necklace rose and fell with my chest's breathing. When I looked back into the mirror, the glow was gone.

"Did you see…" I muttered, trailing off. Squinting, I leaned closer to the mirror, only inches away. Still, I couldn't see a thing.

"See what?" Rhi asked, her eyebrows creased as she watched me nervously look into the mirror from different angles, as if it were a hologram.

But it was gone. And I looked like a fool. Yes. Without a doubt, I was going crazy. *Someone lock me up and throw away the key because I was on my way to loonyville.*

"Nothing," I mumbled, holding the locket in my palm as I wondered what the heck I just saw, and why I kept seeing it.

Chapter 2:

Bite

"I want them gone!" I shouted, the frustration building.

"I'm trying," Rhi said, her voice growing in irritation at my behavior. "But you have a lot of curls." Her fingers worked through the kinks, tugging and pulling them apart. Though, it didn't work.

Yes. I was acting like a child, but I was just so excited about the dance. The boy. I wanted to look pretty, like the other girls. For once, I wanted to feel normal. But at that moment, I felt more like the pumpkin than Cinderella!

"Why do I get cursed with the curls while you get the pretty, straight hair?" I whined, crossing my arms. "It's not fair." She jerked my hair a little harder and I winced, frowning at her in the reflection.

With pursed lips, she sprayed my hair with detangler, brushing through it for the millionth time. And—surprise, surprise—the brush got stuck. Again.

"Maybe I should brush it," I offered, reaching my hand out. She plopped the brush into my hand, and I got to work, weaving my fingers through my hair to detangle the knots. She would never understand. She had the perfect type of hair. Curly, wavy, straight—whatever she wanted, she could do. And her hair would comply because it was good hair.

My hair, on the other hand, was a rebellious little jerk that refused to do anything but frizz.

I threw the brush onto the table, sliding down further into my seat. "Finished," I grumbled, crossing my arms again.

Rhi placed a hand on my shoulder, and I looked up into her radiant topaz eyes, searching for an answer, begging her to tell me how to be a normal girl. She smiled reassuringly and told me to sit up. I obliged.

Then, my darling sister pushed past my bratty behavior and helped me to style my hair. Because my hair was all poof, it was difficult to manage—but not impossible! Rhi had the magic touch.

An hour later, my hair was styled to perfection. Using some concoction of coconut oil, special-order conditioner, and some other stuff I didn't bother asking about, she transformed my hair from the frizzy nightmare that haunted my dreams to the luscious curls I wouldn't mind having. And they were softer. My hair looked silky, like a model's.

My curls cascaded over my shoulder like a Renaissance portrait, pinned over part of my face, covering my scar—she had my gratitude for that. I didn't want any reminder of my former self. Tonight, I was someone different, someone new.

She had pinned little flowers throughout my hair, and I donned a flower headband to match.

All week long, I'd overheard Rachel and her gaggle talk about dressing up as fairies for the Homecoming dance, which doubled as a Halloween dance. Everyone would be in costumes. I wanted to be a fairy, too, but all I could find in our attic was some old masquerade gown and mask.

So, I went with it.

"Now, for the *pièce de résistance,*" she said, sliding the mask onto my face, covering my burn even more. With the gown, the mask, and the hair, I looked like a completely different person. I looked like an ordinary girl!

No, that wasn't right. Because even I could admit that I looked far from ordinary. Dare I say, stunning? Almost.

Turning my head in the reflection, I looked at every angle of her masterpiece. Rhiannon really was an artist, and I could see why she was going to school for art. Though, I couldn't help teasing her as I stared at my reflection with my mouth gaped, in total shock at the transformation. "You should be a hairdresser."

She snorted, shaking her head. "Nah. People like their hairdressers too much."

Such an odd comment but I shrugged it off.

"Now, close your eyes and mouth, because I'm pulling out the hair spray," she said, and I squeezed my eyes shut. "We have a million bobby pins in your hair. If we lose one, it could mean game over, so we're backing up with reinforcements."

I chuckled, closing my mouth tight, preparing myself.

And then she sprayed. And sprayed. Oh, and sprayed some more. So much so that my mother came down the hall, coughing and choking. I opened my eyes to see a mist of hair spray covering the room, my mother waving her hand through the air to clear it out.

"That's enough hair spray to thin the ozone," my mom said, walking past us to open the window and waft the chemicals out with her hands.

"It was a teenage emergency, Mother," Rhi said, capping the spray and shoving it back on the shelf above her vanity.

When my mother pulled her attention from the window, she looked me over, tilting her head as she put on her "mom" face. You know, the one that a mom has when she sees her kid walk for the first time, start kindergarten, or in this case, the first date.

"Oh, baby," she cooed, stepping toward me with open arms. "You look beautiful."

"I agree," Rhiannon said, stepping between us before my mother could embrace me. "Tink looks amazing, thanks to *moi*, but all of this," she motioned to my hair with the brush in her hand, "took over an hour. Hugs can wait until after the dance."

Mom rolled her eyes and shot me a wink, walking back out the door. "Fine, but I'm getting pictures, and that is final."

I groaned, silently pleased to have a typical mother-daughter before-a-dance moment.

Rhi patted the chair, teasing me with the annoying nickname she'd forced onto me. One that she knew I hated. "You're ready to go, Tink."

I rolled my eyes, standing from the chair. She followed behind me as I walked down the stairs toward the front door for my shoes. My mother popped out of her room with an old camera. Was that a Polaroid? What happened to taking pictures on cell phones?

She held up the camera and I posed, the picture coming out slowly. She whipped it from the camera shaking it as she declared she needed 10 more.

Ah, heck. Might as well give the woman what she wanted. It was such a rare occasion, after all. Pose, snap, shake. Pose, snap, shake. Nearly a dozen more times until Rhi said, "Enough! Move over so I can get some on a camera from this century."

"So when is he coming?" Mom asked as Rhi snapped a few pictures of her own. She leaned closer, scrolling through them, mumbling which one should be my profile picture.

"Oh, he's not," I answered absently, looking at the pictures on Rhi's phone. My mother looked at me like I'd just slapped her. So offended and confused. "I'm meeting him at the dance."

"What kind of a date doesn't even pick the girl up?" Rhi grumbled, shoving her phone into her pocket. "Come on, I'll give you a ride."

"Thank you!" I reached in for a hug, but she pushed me away. "Hugging can wait until after the dance," I recited, receiving an approving nod from her. She didn't want anything to ruin the illusion, the magic she'd bestowed upon me in the form of a gorgeous hairstyle, dressed to perfection.

On the ride to school, I began to doubt the entire date. Why *didn't* he pick me up? Was he afraid to come to my house? Afraid of the weird family in the old house that stood alone. Did he believe all the rumors?

He hadn't even spoken to me throughout the week. Only that initial invitation, and then nothing more. Maybe Rhi was right, and he wasn't sincere.

But he seemed so nice…

I had been so excited just to be asked, I didn't think it through. What if I'd been duped? Stood up? What if he was planning to humiliate me in front of the rest of the school? Maybe Rachel put him up to it.

Question after question went off in my mind like little explosions of self-doubt. And I stood in the middle of the minefield, barely escaping the negativity. So much so that I started voicing my concerns, sputtering nonsensical questions faster than I could piece them together.

Rhiannon pulled up to the school and parked the car. She looked at me, waiting for me to finish word vomiting all over the place. When I finally took a breath, she asked, "Are you done?"

I paused for a moment and nodded.

"Great, because you have nothing to worry about, Is. He's probably just an idiot who didn't think to pick his date up at the house. I'll bet he's waiting for you inside right now," she said, gesturing to the school. "And even if this isn't the guy of your dreams, even if you're being 'duped,'" she quoted with her fingers, "you deserve to have a good night."

I took in her words, the possibility that I would walk into that dance and make a total fool of myself. But Rhi's smile that held so much warmth, her eyes that had that genuine squint of happiness, let me know I'd be okay.

"Go on," she said. "Go into that dance and have a great night—with or without a guy. Drink the god-awful punch and dance."

I nodded, still hesitant to open the door. "Just sucks that I have to do it alone. I wish you could go in there with me."

Rhi sighed, grabbing my hand. "I know. I wish I could, too. But this is one of those moments in life where you have to put your big-girl panties on and go in there with your chin held high. You are awesome, and anyone who's worth your time will see that. And anyone who doesn't…" she shrugged. "Screw 'em."

I let out a nervous laugh and opened the car door, swinging my legs out. "Thanks, Rhi. I'll let you know if I need a ride back."

"No problem," she answered, saluting me. "I'll be home if you need me."

Shutting the car door, I stepped up to the big double-door entrance to the school. Those doors stood so dauntingly, daring me to come in. I was tempted to turn around and head back to the car. If Jack asked about it on Monday, I'd tell him I was sick. But I knew Rhi wouldn't let me back in, and I'd be forced to walk home or walk into the dance, so I did as she said. I pulled on my metaphorical big-girl pants and pushed open those doors, determined to have a great night.

The music blared as soon as I opened the doors. *Jeez, talk about soundproof...*

Colorful lights blinked and fluttered, moving across the gym. Decorations of spiders, witches, ghouls, ghosts, vampires, fairies—pretty much anything Halloween—riddled the gym. Orange and black garlands hung from the snack and drink tables, streamers dipping low from the ceilings and hanging from the walls.

The speakers pounded with a deep bass, girls bounced their butts to the music hoping to impress their dates with their seductive moves. It only made me want to laugh because they were anything but seductive. They were teenagers, like me, trying to look like grown women—and failing miserably. But their dates were oblivious, being teenage boys and all, and were pleased with the attention.

But that begged the question—where was my date? And would I end up attempting the same dance of seduction as them?

Not in a million years. I'd be lucky if I could make it through the night without stuttering too much when I spoke.

Students wore a variety of costumes—some skimpier than others, while some took the humorous approach. Maybe I should have asked him what he'd be wearing. At this point, I'd have to get a good look at the costumes to tell which he was.

My eyes scanned over Rachel and her friends with their dates. So, they went for the skimpier approach. Or, as much as the school would allow. As planned, the girls were all dressed as fairies, and they were covered in glitter, from their hair to their faces, their colorful make up, and even their costumes. Every time the lights shone over them, they sparkled and glimmered, like real fairies.

Their dates were dressed as vampires. The entire football team, really. Ironic, considering their team was the Hadley bats. But it didn't seem like anyone else was. A few girls had dressed as fairies, but they couldn't dedicate the amount of detail that Rachel and her friends had. The other girls looked like the knock-off version of fairies. The store brand. The cheap costumes you buy at the discount store, an attempt to match up to the desired effect that you just couldn't achieve, so you come out looking second-rate.

It was a good thing I couldn't find a fairy costume, or I'd have looked the same. Though *I* thought they looked great, they didn't compare to Rachel's group and would surely be teased for trying. I felt bad, honestly, because I knew that feeling all too well. Trying too hard to belong, to fit in, but never quite getting there. So close, yet always out of reach.

As expected, Rachel and her band of airheads made fun of those other girls, sneering and cackling like evil fairies—the kind that would eat your face and then laugh about it.

I missed my Halloweens from childhood with Rhi. When we could trick-or-treat and no one would know it was us. Costumes and masks hid us, helped us blend in with the other kids. And for that one night every year, we were normal kids.

Hopefully, this mask on my face could work that same magic.

Rachel's eyes locked onto mine. I tried to turn away, to get some punch, but it was too late. Target had been identified, and she was ready to strike. But it was her shrill, "Eww!" that stood out the most.

I took a deep breath and turned to face her, wearing an unamused expression as I waited for her taunting to pass.

"I think that's the scariest costume I've seen all night," Rachel shouted; Amanda laughed loudly behind her. "Oh, wait. It's just Isabel." She stepped closer, her face less than a foot from mine, and her eyes narrowed into slits. "Don't think that a mask can cover that hideous burn."

Holding back my reaction, I just stared at her, refusing to answer. Not like I could as my stomach was doing flips and turns, making me so nauseated, I thought I might spew. But I swallowed hard and pretended they didn't faze me. They were just looking for a way to exclude me so they could feel superior.

"Where's your date?" Amanda sneered, hands on her hips.

"He probably ran off when he caught a glimpse of that," Rachel laughed, pointing her thumb at me.

I looked around but couldn't see him in the crowd. *Please, oh please, do not let me get stood up.* Looking away, my shoulders slumped, ready to accept defeat. But a hand on my shoulder startled me, followed by a male voice.

"That's no way to talk to my date, ladies," the guy said, giving my shoulder a light squeeze. *My hero! My knight in shining armor.* I swore I could kiss…

Wesley? I turned to see my savior, and it was the new kid in town.

"Now why don't you go back to Danny, Rachel. He's waiting for you by the punch bowl."

Rachel scoffed, stomping her foot before stalking off in another direction—her little ducklings following closely behind.

I glanced back at Wesley, who wore a charming smile. The kind of smile that melted my insides to goo. It encompassed his sweet, yet daring, personality. "Wesley?" I asked, my tone breathless with a bit of shock.

"Are you disappointed?" he asked, cocking an eyebrow.

Disappointed? Though he was new, everyone loved Wesley. He played on the football team and got along great with those guys. But he was also kind to the other kids in school. The ones who were generally excluded, like me. He treated everyone with respect, which made everyone love him even more.

I shook my head, my words coming out a jumbled mess. "No, I—it's not that I'm disappointed. Who would be dis… It's just that I thought you were… You know what? Thanks. Thank you for sticking up for me."

He chuckled, casting me that charming smile. "Rachel can stand to be knocked down a peg or two." He leaned closer, saying in a hushed tone, "If she keeps scowling like that, her face will get stuck that way."

There was no suppressing the laughter that escaped me—though I wished I could've sounded a bit less like a donkey. But it was nice to hear someone else voice those things about Rachel. Everyone else worried too much they'd risk their status on the social hierarchy if they did, but Wesley didn't care. He was being true to himself and his own opinions. It was refreshing. And the way he'd leaned in as he said it, it felt like we shared our own little secret.

Extending a hand, he asked, "Would you like to dance?"

Ah, the classic question that every girl died to be asked. And I had to turn him down. "Oh, um… I'm actually waiting on Jack." My face flushed. *Please, tell me he didn't ditch me and I wasn't making a moron of myself by assuming he was waiting. Don't let Rachel be right.*

"He's with the rest of the team by the locker rooms. They'll be out soon."

"Why aren't you with them?"

"They're planning some ridiculous initiation for the new guy—me," he answered, seemingly annoyed with his fellow teammates. "It's bad enough Coach forced us all to dress up like vampires. One uniform is enough. And how dumb do I look as a vampire?"

I gave him a once over, not at all disappointed with what I saw. His dark suit vest pulled tight against his flowy white dress shirt. Paired with his dark pants, he looked much older than he was, as if he really was a vampire who stepped out from another time, another life.

He leaned in closer, his cologne invading my nostrils. But not in the overbearing sense like when the guys in English repeatedly sprayed Old Spice until we all gagged and choked. No, his scent was much softer but held a bite of musk. I closed my eyes for a moment, inhaling before I snapped myself back.

Did he catch that? Based on the clever smile he wore, I'd say yes—but he didn't seem repulsed. If anything, his grin widened, and in a low voice he asked, "So, while we wait for Jack to return from his alcoholic endeavors, would you care to dance?" He extended a gloved hand, and—utterly speechless—I took it.

My first time dancing with a boy. Well, not if you count that time in grade school when I was forced to dance with Rodney Peters for a school play. But this was a real dance. The kind that made my heart flutter in elation while also sinking in anticipation.

I couldn't dance. And I didn't mean that I didn't know any moves, or that my knowledge was limited to the Cha Cha Slide. I mean, I couldn't dance to save my life. Ask Wesley's poor toes. I stepped on them repeatedly, muttering an apology every time. My only savior was that it was a slow song, so we didn't move very much.

Still, every time he assured me that it was fine. But my lack of grace left me humiliated and bright red.

Unable to look him in the eyes, I stared down at my gown I kept tripping over. His hand slid to my back, making me jump a little. He pulled me a little closer and whispered, "Relax." The word rolled off his tongue, assuring me to let go of the pressure.

So I did.

And I had fun. When I stopped trying to dance well, I loosened up enough to actually not step on his feet a billion times. I was able to laugh and make jokes with him in a way that I hadn't done with anyone outside of my family. But Wesley was different. He was carefree and kind. He treated me like a person. For a moment, I forgot all about Jack.

Until he *finally* made his appearance, swooping in like James Bond and slithering his arm around my waist. But there was something different in the way his hand felt against my back than Wesley's had. It made me nervous and slightly uncomfortable.

But I let him. If I pulled away now, I risked losing any attention from him and go back to being that weird loner girl. The one whose family is in a cult, or are Satanic witches, or whatever else people made up about us.

I didn't want to go back to being that girl. Not when I'd tasted the sweet fruit from the other side of the fence. In one week, I'd found two people to add to my socials. *I'll be an influencer in no time.* I could've scoffed aloud at the thought. *As if…*

"Thanks for keeping my date company, Wes." He winked, pulling me from Wesley's kind touch to his more persistent one. It all happened so fast, neither of us had time to react. I wasn't used to having the attention of one guy, let alone two. And now I was being tugged away, my body tensing up like a twig.

Wesley's eyes narrowed slightly, a look of disappointment on his face. Nodding, he said, "Anytime, man." He took a step toward me, his voice low once more as he said, "You were a lovely partner," before turning and walking away.

A pang of guilt shot through my chest. I'd enjoyed his company. Genuinely enjoyed it. And after he defended me from Rachel and danced with me as I waited, I allowed myself to be swooped away like it was nothing. Jack was the one that kept me waiting. I should be mad, right? Wouldn't one of the other girls be mad if their date didn't even show up for the first half hour?

But here I stood, a pathetic trophy on his arm, happy that I wasn't stood up. I should have told Wesley he was a good partner, too. Or that he was a great guy and I liked his company. *Something.* But instead, I let him walk away.

Jack pulled me into his body, his arm now loosely draped around my shoulder, pulling me along as we neared the others—the football team and their dates.

"Ooohh," they called out, seeing us walking so closely together. As if we were a couple.

And honestly, I liked it!

A bashful smile covered my face as I watched the team bump arms and playfully push each other around, all while their dates stood nearby, rolling their eyes.

Guys…

I stood awkwardly as he chatted with the other guys. Staring around me, my eyes caught Wesley talking with another boy from the chess team. They shared a laugh as they drank the overly sugared, watery punch.

A shrill voice from one of the girls pulled my attention back to the group as they talked about a party or something. Maybe I should pay attention in case I get invited. Being with Jack, I had that chance.

Before I knew it, the group dispersed to the dance floor, and Jack pulled me even closer, until I was forced to wrap my arm around his back.

"The guys wanted me to go to that after-party, but I told them no," he said, his face closer to mine than anyone else had ever been.

"Oh?"

"Yeah," he answered, swiping his hair back with his other hand. "I told them we had plans."

That caught me off guard. I hadn't in a million years expected him to say that. But god, was I flattered! *What if he wants to be alone because he wants to kiss me?* Would I be getting my first kiss tonight? The thought filled me with both terror and excitement.

He looked at me, his gaze holding intrigue, and he leaned closer, his lips nearly touching my ears. "You want to get out of here?"

Pulling away, he looked at me, waiting for my answer.

Did I want to leave? I don't know—yes? No? I'd heard the other girls talk about what happened with boys in cars. I'd watched TV, read books, and knew the possibilities—both good and bad. Maybe he wanted to take a drive, talk a little. Maybe he wanted to make out. Or, maybe he wanted more. But this was my one shot to feel normal.

I nodded. "Sure." Though, my voice was barely above a whisper.

His grin widened, and using his arm around me, he led me out of the school and to his car. I waited to see if he'd open the door—like they did in the movies—but he headed straight for the driver's seat. What else should I expect from someone who didn't even bother to pick me up from the house? But I was too fascinated, too invested, to think anything more of it.

I got into the car, strapped myself in, and he pulled out. "What do you think of the car?" he asked, driving away from the school and toward the park.

"It's nice," I answered, forcing enthusiasm. All I knew was that it was a sporty, red car. So, when he started talking about all the parts and features that Danny helped him install, I was lost. He could've been speaking French, and I wouldn't have known the difference. Still, I nodded along, smiling.

When he finished talking about his car, he asked me about my family. Did he really not know the rumors? Or was he being nice and playing stupid? Hopefully, he wasn't planning to tease me. If he hung out with Rachel, there would be no way he'd never heard of *the crazies on the edge of town*, as she put it.

"I live with my mother and sister. You might know my sister, Rhiannon. She went to our school last year."

He neither confirmed nor denied if he did, but I kept talking anyway. "She's in college now, but she still lives at home."

"Where's your dad?"

I looked away. "My dad is gone. I don't really know much about him, but he died when I was a baby."

He glanced over from the driver's side, placing a hand on my knee, offering a look of sympathy.

We pulled into the park, driving along the winding road to the parking lot. When we stepped out of the car, I asked if we were going to sit on the hood, like in the movies. Mostly, I was joking, but the look on his face—the shock that I would even *think* about sitting on the hood of his precious car—let me know that he took me seriously. He led me along the trail, stopping at a bench, where we took a seat.

My poofy masquerade dress was a challenge to maneuver, but Jack paid me no mind as I got settled on the bench. Why *was* he bringing me to the park? Maybe we were here for a romantic evening in the woods, surrounded by nature. I did love nature and felt most comfortable surrounded by it.

His arm stretched along the bench behind me, nearly wrapped around my shoulders. Sheepishly, I looked up at him, at his handsome features and devilish grin. "Do you have to check in with your mom or anything?"

"No. I'll just text her later." I figured she wouldn't care if I left the dance. It's not like this was an everyday occurrence, so even if I did get lectured for not calling sooner, it'd be worth the lecture. I'd just think about Jack's face the entire time, that wickedly handsome grin.

With a satisfied smile, he looked me up and down, saying, "You look good in that dress. Mouth-watering."

Did he just lick his lips?

Heat flushed my cheeks, not feeling entirely comfortable with the action, but the attention outweighed the discomfort. The desire to experience what the other girls did was why I answered with a smitten, "Oh, I don't know. The other girls looked pretty in their fairy costumes."

He scoffed. "Fairies. What a simple-minded choice. But *you* look like the girl who would be on a vampire's arm." He slid closer until our hips were nearly touching as we sat beside one another.

I gulped, trying to suppress the excitement building in my chest, pushing away the uneasiness. "Do you... really think so?"

"Oh yeah," he answered, leaning in closer as he brushed my semi-tamed hair behind my ear. His mouth hovered over my neck, sending a shiver through my body, extending to my limbs. He inhaled deeply, his voice smooth as he whispered, "Do you know why I wanted to be here with you? Why it had to be you?"

My eyes fluttered closed, allowing myself to feel the moment with every one of my senses: the way the air felt on that crisp October evening, or how he smelled so masculine, wearing cologne that was much better than the cheap bottles the guys excessively sprayed in class. This was my first real date, and it was with a guy who was more man than a boy—and in turn, he made me feel more woman than girl. Maybe that sounded silly or juvenile, but I didn't care. I leaned into the moment, preparing myself for what I thought might be my first kiss.

"Why me?" I asked, my voice breathless.

"I needed a loser," he answered, his tone taking on something darker and cruel.

My eyes popped open, and I pulled away from him, shaking my head. *Did I hear that right?* My heart sank, knowing deep down that it was too good to be true. *Of course. Someone like me will never get a moment like this.* Tears brimmed my eyes, knowing that any semblance of hope had vanished.

"I needed someone no one would care about, and you were the perfect target. No friends, no father, mother and sister town outcasts... You think they'd miss you if you were gone?"

Tears fell silently down my cheeks, and I looked away, anger slowly bubbling inside me. But the disappointment was too much.

He cackled, a cruel mockery of the loser girl who was stupid enough to think she had a chance. Brushing my hair back from my neck, I winced at the touch, but he held me firm. "No, no," he warned. "Hold still and this will be over soon."

My heart pounded furiously in my chest, uncertain of what he'd meant. *What was he planning to do with me?*

His tongue grazed over the nape of my neck, and I shoved him away, shouting, "Get off!" No way would he do… *whatever* he was thinking about doing. No. Not after the things he'd said, the way he'd broken me.

But his hold on me was too strong. Grabbing my shoulders, he held me in place with unmatched strength. He tilted his head toward me, and that was when I noticed… *fangs*, glistening in the moonlight. "Hold still," he grumbled, struggling to hold me as I fought back.

My locket began to glow, enough of a shock for him to loosen his grip and back up. "What the—" he barely got those words out before a sudden force blew him backward, his butt landing on the ground.

Stumbling to his feet, he stood straight, but the locket glowed brighter until it reached a blinding light.

His skin sizzled from the light, his body melting away before bursting into a large flame, nearly eight feet tall in height.

Screaming in agony, he slowly crumpled to the ground—or, what was left of him—before his body simply disintegrated into dust.

My mouth gaped wide open, jaw to the ground. How the— what the— *Huh?* What the *hell* did I just see? Was that real? It had to be, right? No, it couldn't be. Could it? It didn't make sense, but I'd witnessed it with my own eyes. Maybe I really was crazy.

I was too stunned to speak or scream. The only thought that came to mind was *run*.

So, I did.

I ran down the trail in the opposite direction of his ugly red car. I ran until I reached the road, and then I ran some more.

The adrenaline—the pure fear that claimed me—was more than enough to fuel me. I couldn't even feel the exhaustion in my legs, the sting in my lungs that begged for more oxygen.

Was he trying to bite me? Did he really have a fang? Was he planning to kill me? How did he burn alive? Did my locket do that?

The entire run back, questions riddled my mind, a puzzle I just couldn't solve, each one leaving me more panicked than the last.

I passed people walking along the sidewalk in town, unfazed by a young woman running down the street in distress—because what they saw was a Dufort and kept their distance.

Finally, I reached my street. The empty road would usually give me solace but not that night. Not in the darkness, after such terror. It only made my fear heighten.

I didn't know what to do or think. All I could do was run.

Chapter 3:

Legacy

I burst through the front door, pieces of twigs and leaves stuck in my poofy hair. Plucking out a few, I tossed them to the floor, shutting the door behind me.

"What's going on?" my mother asked, rushing toward me. My dress was torn, stained with the same dust and dirt that covered my face and arms. My mask was gone, pulled off by a branch on my hasty run home.

Rhiannon stood on one side, my mother on the other, both waiting for me to explain why I came in looking like I'd been to the end of the Earth and back. But I was too shocked to speak. Too confused. Uncertain I witnessed what I had. All I could do was mutter nonsense.

"He... blew up. Explosion... Boom... And his...pieces of him... he turned to dust. The locket... blew him up..." I motioned with my hands, still trying to catch my breath.

My mother looked at me, and then at Rhiannon. "I'll go make her some tea. See if you can figure out what happened."

Rhiannon grabbed my hand, looking me in the eyes. "Isabel, breathe. Calm down. Explain to me what happened."

"He's dead. Jack is dead," I said, regaining my composure a bit now that I'd settled down a little inside the safety of my home. Being surrounded by the only two people who cared about me made me feel protected, like nothing bad would happen. It gave me a moment to relax a little and replay what had happened with a clearer mind.

A few minutes later, my mother returned with a mug of peppermint green tea. She knew how much I loved the peppermint from the garden.

"Come on, Tink, talk to me," Rhi said, her tone filled with concern. *If only she knew how crazy I really was...* They led me to the couch, my mother sitting on the chair across from me, Rhiannon at my side.

"Jack... he tried to hurt me. I think he wanted to bite me. I don't know—it all happened so fast. He tried to attack me, but the locket started glowing, and it made him explode into dust."

Yup. Definitely crazy. There was no way anyone would believe it. *I* didn't believe it, and it happened to *me*!

I shook my head, looking down at the floor. "I know I sound crazy, but I swear—"

"No," Rhiannon said, placing her hand on my arm and giving it a light, reassuring squeeze. "We believe you." She looked to our mother and said, "It's time, Mom."

Confused, I looked back and forth between them, at the shared glances they exchanged, holding a secret that I had a hunch would change my life drastically. Based on their expressions, whatever they were about to say was big.

"Drink your tea first, honey," Mom said, nodding with a smile.

I looked to Rhiannon, who also nodded along.

I was beginning to think maybe our family *was* a cult, and I was about to sip the red Kool-Aid. The tea was steaming, and I blew on it before taking a sip. The warm liquid ran down my throat, leaving a trail of comfort all the way to my belly. When the mug was halfway empty, I set it down and asked, "What's going on?"

My mother was calm. Far calmer than she should have been after her daughter was attacked. Why? Why wasn't she more frantic, more confused, more concerned?

"Isa, honey," she said, her tone soft, and I knew that meant she was trying to butter me up, to make me feel at ease. *Just spit it out, already!* "The rumors you've heard about our family... Well, they aren't entirely false."

Here I was making jokes in my mind about drinking the Kool-Aid, and it was all true. "We really are a cult?" I asked, my eyes landing on the mug I'd just sipped from.

"What? No." My mother chuckled, shaking her head. "We're witches, sweetheart."

Oh, because that made much more sense. The way she said it—as if I was silly for thinking we were members of a cult when the obvious answer was witchcraft—had me gaping in disbelief. At least a cult was real. Witchcraft was what normal people called a bunch of hocus pocus.

Was she mocking me? Lying? Was this some elaborate prank they'd put together?

Between running so far and everything that happened with Jack, my head was pounding. The peppermint tea wasn't helping the nausea that had claimed my stomach, churning and twisting it like my intestines were a towel being wrung out.

And to top it all off, I hadn't even begun to think about the disappointment of knowing that Rachel was right, after all. He wasn't interested in me.

I blew out a frustrated sign. "What are you talking about, Mom?"

"We're witches. You have magical powers."

Rhiannon rubbed my arm soothingly and said, "That's why Jack burned up. The locket is a conduit of magical power, and it saved you from his attack."

"By killing him!" I shouted, jerking my arm from her touch. "Isn't that a little extreme?"

"Not necessarily," Rhiannon answered. "He was a vampire."

I laughed, though there was not an ounce of humor. "Oh, he was a vampire. Okay, that makes sense. And Mr. Jenkins down the road is a troll, right?"

Rhi rolled her eyes, scoffing. "Get real, Tink."

My jaw clenched; her response only grew my irritation. "No, *you* get real, Rhiannon! You guys are telling me we're witches, and you expect me to believe it? To believe we have *magical powers* and kill vampires? And let me guess, these magical powers," I quoted with my fingers, "are also the reason I've been seeing weird things in the mirror?"

Mom and Rhi looked at each other, their eyebrows creased and pulled in tight. "Seeing things?" they asked in sync.

"Yeah. I swear, I've been going crazy, seeing these weird images in the mirror. Really sick stuff. People eating other people, blood everywhere— it's bad."

"Why didn't you tell us?" Rhi asked, her expression softened, her tone kinder.

Had she had visions, too? Is that why she was being so nice?

"Tell you what?" I asked, choking on my words. I threw my arms up in defeat. "Tell you that I'm crazy? That I'm seeing beyond disturbing images? I don't believe it myself!" Everything was too much. Too freaking much! I couldn't handle it anymore. Between school and home, my life had become a freaking nightmare!

I grunted loudly in frustration, my voice high-pitched, cracking in the middle. The lights in the room flickered, the tables and lamps trembling and shaking lightly, like an earthquake that was just enough to make its presence known but not enough to destroy anything.

My eyes grew wide, and I scooted back in my seat as far as I could. Rhi rubbed my arm in a soothing motion again, calming me down. "It's okay, Isa. Deep breath and hold for three seconds."

I shook my head, not even interpreting her words, but she repeated them, nonetheless.

"Breathe deep and hold."

After a moment, it settled in and I took a deep breath, holding and then blowing it out. Again. And again. Until the furniture's shaking steadied and stopped. The mug had tipped over, spilling the rest of my tea on the table. Tea ran down the side, dripping onto the carpet below.

"That was your magic surfacing," my mother said, extending her hand and snapping her finger. A towel hovered over to her. With her finger motioning up and down, the hovering towel dabbed the spot in time with her motion.

I watched in awe, utterly speechless.

"You're a teenager," she said as she continued cleaning, like she hadn't just made a towel fly over and clean the carpet. "Your emotions are all over the place, which can intensify the magic. It was manifesting through visions and, just now, through the furniture. And tonight, when that boy tried to attack you, the fear and anger made your magic surge."

It was all too much to take in, so I just sat there like a lump, unable to speak or think. I could barely take her words in. It was as if they hovered in the air, waiting to be accepted, but I was shooing them away.

My mother knew this. She knew me too well. So, she continued explaining, knowing my brain would bounce back in a minute when it all sunk in.

"Our family has been protecting this town for generations. You see, there are other supernatural beings who want to harm people. Vampires. In a sense, you could call us vampire hunters. We see the threat and take it out, protecting people. They must not know what we are, so we protect them while living under the guise of being outcasts—someone they wouldn't expect to fight the monsters that lurk in the closet."

I scoffed, crossing my arms. "Why? Why should we help them when they treat us so horribly?"

"Because we are gifted with the power of enchantment. With that power comes obligation. We can't be given something so precious and waste it. We are expected to use that power to benefit humanity."

Rhiannon nodded, adding, "Like in *Spiderman*. 'With great power comes great responsibility.'"

I snorted a laugh at the thought. She was comparing this to Spiderman—an obviously made-up story—to relate to being a witch, something you'd think would also be made up but apparently wasn't.

"But why *us?* I mean, what makes us so special?" I asked, my mind pulled in every direction, conflicted.

On one hand, being a witch was compelling. I always thought it looked so cool on TV when people had magic. I'd be lying if I said I never wanted it for myself. But this? This was different. Aside from my fantasies, I'd always wanted to fit in. To belong with the other kids, feel like I was part of the group. Having magic excluded me from that possibility.

My mother leaned forward, her butt raised off her chair as she grabbed my hand, using her thumb to caress a calming circle on my palm. "Oh, baby," she cooed, her eyes soft and filled with compassion. "I know it's a lot to take in, but this is the truth. We are witches, and we have a responsibility to uphold. That responsibility requires great sacrifice. For our family, that means we must remain outsiders to the rest of the town."

My head jerked toward her, tilted in confusion—eyebrows creased so hard, they brought my headache back. "What do you mean? I'm like this on purpose?"

She took a deep breath and nodded. "Our power is strengthened through our exclusion. I'm not sure why it is like that, but it has been for generations. The more the town hates and fears us, the stronger we are. And we use that power to protect them by helping them in secret."

The words struck me, and I remembered earlier that week when I returned Rachel's phone in secret. Was that what she meant by a family trait? That helping people was ingrained in us?

"That's why I started the rumors about us years ago. By having the town shun us, I hoped it would give me enough power to keep them safe on my own. At least until you guys were old enough to help me. And now you both are!"

She was actually excited, as if I'd hit a milestone. Maybe I had, but it felt like it was anything but a milestone. It was like reliving when I got my first period: Everyone said I was a *woman* and that it was a great thing, but really, I wanted to curl up with my heating pad as I ate chocolate all week and cried at sad movies. How was that a great thing?

This innate desire to help people was not a blessing. It was a curse.

How could they do this? How could they keep something like this from me? "Why didn't you tell me?" I asked, directing my question to Rhi more than my mother. "I thought we were close, Rhi! How could you keep something *this major* a secret from me?"

Rhi shifted uncomfortably—a move so subtle and minute, no one else would notice but me. Because I knew my sister.

Or, I thought I did.

Anger bubbled inside me, burning through my body like a raging inferno, ready to destroy everything within my touch.

"You lied!" I shouted, jumping up from the couch and pointing an accusatory finger at my sister. Then, to my mother. My heart beat rapidly, pushing me closer to the breaking point. "I've always told you everything, and you lied to me!"

"We did it for your own good," Rhi pleaded, but I refused to believe a word she said. At that moment, she was nothing more than a liar, and I needed to get away from them both.

"That's a bullshit answer, and you know it," I said, charging up the stairs to my own sanctuary. The one place I could be alone.

"Isabel, wait!" my mother cried, running to the bottom of the stairs, but my sister told her to let me be.

At least she could do one thing right.

I ran into my room, grabbed my pillow, and screamed into it, needing some kind of release. Tears filled my eyes, pouring out. And as though someone had turned on a faucet, they flowed, unrelenting.

They said we had power? Ha! I'd never felt more powerless than I did in that moment—the utter helplessness of my life. I'd tried to be like the others, to blend in and be a member of the pack. That failed miserably. Turned into an eat-or-be-eaten situation. My first date and he attacked me and disintegrated before my very eyes.

Why couldn't he have just stood me up?

Like it could even be considered a date. He only wanted me there because even he could tell that I was a loser. Pathetic.

And now, I had another thing to alienate me from everyone else: to learn that my isolation from my peers had been because of *her*...

Grabbing the pillow, I screamed again; the pillow muffling the sound. I sat down on the bed, my head hung in defeat. A soft brush against my hand startled me.

"Biscuits," I sobbed, grabbing the cat and snuggling into him.

He didn't really belong to us. The black cat had just shown up on the porch one day and hung around. When Rhi and I first saw him, we tossed him a few biscuits, and he ate them up, so we started calling him Biscuits. He was almost protective over us, hissing at anyone else who came across his path. And in that moment, I needed the comfort of this strange cat. I needed his protection—as crazy as it sounded.

After about an hour of stewing, there was a soft knock on my door. "Come in," I grumbled, not bothering to get up from my spot on the bed. I was still too bitter.

"You're not going to hurl a book at me, are you?" Rhiannon teased, peeking past the door for a dramatic effect.

I tsked, rolling my eyes.

Sighing, she walked over and sat down beside me. "Tink, I'm sorry I didn't tell you about our family's... *unique* qualities."

"That's one word for it," I mumbled, crossing my arms.

"Trust me, I wanted to tell you as soon as I found out, but Mom said we needed to wait."

"So what? I thought we told each other everything! This was big, Rhi, and you hid it from me."

"Well, at least I'm here for you now! Try finding out and having to go through it alone, with only Mom to help you. It sucked! I had to keep it a secret from everyone. You, my friends, even Kevin. Remember him?"

"Your old boyfriend, Kevin?"

"Yeah. Remember how close we were? I couldn't tell him, and it killed me to hide something so personal about myself from him and my friends. But knowing it was my responsibility to keep them safe, I had to give up my popularity to do so. I made that choice because I cared about them. And now you'll have to make that choice, too."

She cast me a reassuring smile, stepping out of my room to leave me with those words floating through the air, testing me and weighing heavily on my mind.

After everything that happened, I was exhausted. Standing in front of the mirror, I wiped my face clean of makeup, smudging it more than cleaning it off. Why was taking it off just as hard as putting it on? *Great, now I look like a raccoon.*

With a frustrated grunt, I threw the tissues into the trash and sat at the edge of my bed, staring into the mirror. As I watched, my locket began to glow, the reflection shining bright against the surface of the mirror.

Once again, within the glow was an image. Leaning closer, I watched the scene unfold. The people, boys it looked like, were all dressed in cloaks. It looked as if they were being initiated in some kind of ritual as they all stood in a circle.

Though it was brief, the image burned into my mind before it disappeared. The glare from the locket shrunk to nothing, the image vanishing in an instant. I almost doubted I'd seen anything at all, and had it been even a few days earlier, I would have. Knowing what I do now, I knew the image was real.

Turning away, I flopped onto my bed. My hands clung to my forehead, rubbing my temple as I squeezed my eyes shut. I needed something different—something to make my life anything but what it was now. A change. *Something!*

A growl from Biscuits startled me. My eyes shot open to look at the black cat sitting on my windowsill. His back was arched as he stared out the window, focused on something outside.

Cocking my head to the side, I got up from bed to glance out the window. I couldn't see anything with the light on, so I turned it off to look again. Yet, I saw nothing but the woods. Still, Biscuits growled, the hair on his back raised, his tail flicking furiously.

I shook my head and climbed into bed, slowly drifting off. As I lay there, flowing in and out of sleep, I heard a tune. An ominous, unfamiliar tune. One that felt entirely too foreboding. Too *real* to be a dream.

Chapter 4:

Drained

"I'm tired of being this frizzy-haired weirdo all the time," I said to Rhi as I struggled with dying the tips of my hair. "I want a change."

No longer did I want to be the weird girl, the loser. I wanted more. And by god, I would get it myself if I had to. So, like any female facing a mental breakdown—I decided to change my hair.

Rhi looked at me, concerned and conflicted.

If I dyed my hair, I might actually start to belong. Then where would their precious magic be? Oh, well. They'd gone this long without my magic, why would they need it now?

"You can either help or leave, but I'm not backing out now, Rhi. I'm dyeing my tips."

"The tips, huh?" Rhi smirked, closing the bathroom door behind me and telling me to grab a towel. "First of all, you can't do this without at least two towels. Not unless you want Mom to go mental when she sees pink hair dye stained on everything."

I smiled, grabbing two towels. "Alright, what's next?" Eagerly, I bounced from one leg to the other, unable to contain my excitement.

This was happening. I was really about to dye my hair.

"Why only the tips?" Rhi asked, handing me the brush. She wasn't about to attempt brushing my hair again—not after last time.

I shrugged, yanking the brush through a stubborn curl, forcing the knots away with sheer willpower and anticipation. "I could only afford one kit, and my hair is too thick to dye it all. According to the box, anyway."

Rhi stepped around me, observing my hair. "Hmm… I think the box was right. We'd probably need three bottles for all this hair," she teased, grabbing a chunk of curl and holding it out.

I finished brushing through my hair and she told me to sit still while she applied the dye. Mixing the two bottles together and shaking vigorously—as the directions said—she held up a thick strand, meeting my gaze in the mirror. "Ready?" I nodded and she squeezed some of the color onto my hair, rubbing it in at the edges.

My eyes kept darting to the clock on the wall, wondering how long the process took. Sure, the box said to let it sit for 40 minutes, but was that from the moment she started applying or finished? Because it was already 10 minutes in, and we'd barely covered half of my hair. I couldn't imagine how long it would take to dye all of it.

We sat in silence for a while, but a question had been gnawing at me the whole time. "Why are you helping me?" I asked.

Her eyes flicked up, looking at me through the reflection in the mirror. "What do you mean?"

"You obviously don't want me to dye my hair. I heard you and Mom talking when I walked in with it. So, why are you helping me dye it?"

She paused, her hands retreating for a moment as she looked away and chewed on her lip—a sure sign that something weighed heavily on her mind.

"I guess, I know you need the support," she answered slowly, as if piecing it together herself. "When I found out about our magic, I didn't have someone to help me through it. Mom was… well, you saw. She was so excited my magic had come in, she didn't even think about how it affected me negatively."

"I know the feeling," I mumbled, hoping it would relieve some of the tension. But Rhiannon forced a laugh.

"You know, I reacted the exact same way you did. I refused to listen to Mom and went through my own rebellious phase. In fact, I have a few clothes in my closet that might fit you a little better than they fit me now."

I perked up at that information. "Really?" I asked excitedly.

"Why not! I can't wear them anymore. Someone might as well get some use out of them. Though, they are a little edgier than the earth tones you wear now." She motioned to my brown suede pants and flowy green shirt that matched the rest of my closet.

"Edgy is fine," I answered. "Edgy is perfect." Anything to make me look different than I did.

Through our conversation, she'd finished dying my tips and it wasn't long until we were washing it out. Afterward, I went to her room, and she helped me pick out a few new outfits for school on Monday.

I felt bold—ready to begin my new life with a new me.

But on Monday morning, that confidence had shriveled faster than a snail in the sunlight.

With a little ego boost from Rhiannon, I put on the outfit we'd planned out together—just like our high school days before she graduated—and I headed out the door.

There was no denying, I was nervous! Not only was I showing up to school an entirely different person, but I had Jack's death looming over me. Anyone with eyes saw us leave the dance together. No doubt, I'd be the prime suspect in his disappearance.

Rhi suggested I ask out another guy. Pretend that Jack dropped me off at home and never called me back—that he ghosted me. Of course, I thought there was no way I could ask someone out, but I remembered how nice Wesley was at the dance. "No problem," I'd told her with a smirk. "I think I know just the guy to ask."

At the time, I felt confident. But now? My nerves were like jelly.

On the way out, I caught a glimpse of my reflection in the car mirror, and I couldn't believe that it was me in that reflection. If it weren't for my poofy red hair, I'd have assumed I was looking at a stranger. But even in the car's reflection, my emerald eyes stood out.

My eyes scanned over my outfit. I'd ditched the brown suede pants and flowy green shirt I typically donned, swapping it out for a black band T-shirt, dark jeans with rips at the knees, and a pair of red boots that Rhiannon let me borrow. Honestly, the entire outfit was hers, but in a weird way, it suited the new me.

When I stepped into the building, my nerves had eaten every shred of confidence I'd stored away—like a squirrel stashing its nuts for the winter. But it was gone. All of it. Suddenly, I wished I'd never made a change. Who was I kidding, no amount of hair dye or cool clothing would make me any less... me.

With my head down, I walked to my locker, grabbing my books for first period. And that's when I heard it... the first murmur.

"Is that the Dufort girl? Oh my God, she looks so different."

"I know. Cool, right?"

"Totally."

Deep breath. They liked it. So far, all good critiques. Maybe this transformation wasn't such a bad idea.

With my chin held a little higher, I headed to first period, whispers of the new me following me everywhere I went.

"She looks so different."

"Is that Isabel? Wow."

"What a total shocker, right?"

Sure, there were a few scoffs or eye rolls, but overall, the change had mostly been met with positivity. And that positivity gave me courage. Enough courage to even speak up in class a bit, engaging in a discussion I would have never engaged in before. And because I felt so confident, so sure, people were talking back. Responding to me with more than taunts and mockery.

I headed to the cafeteria after second period. In the hallway, I saw Wesley standing by the water fountain, waiting for a turn.

Should I go over there? Maybe I could start a conversation. He seemed so nice at the dance. Then again, look what happened with Jack.

But with Wesley, it felt genuine, like he'd meant the things he said, the way he acted. He seemed like an all-around nice guy. At worst, he might shoo me away politely. And honestly, what did I have to lose? It wasn't like my social status could tank any further. Not like I had friends to disappoint or a boyfriend who'd be jealous.

"Hey, Wesley," I choked out, my voice strangled and awkward. Still, he turned and waved.

"Hey, Isabel. How's it going?"

He asked a question back, so that meant he wanted a conversation, right? Or was he just being polite? Only one way to find out…

"Oh, uh, you know. It's, uh, going," I said, my words a jumbled, idiotic mess. "How about you?"

Wesley smiled, stepping closer to me, causing both my heart and my nerves to soar. "Mornings aren't my friend," he teased with a chuckle. "I'm always running late in the morning, so I skipped breakfast again and my stomach's been growling since."

As he said it, his stomach growled again, loud enough to be heard above the hallway ruckus.

I laughed, reaching into my bag for a Pop-Tart I'd grabbed before I left. I'd planned on sneaking a few pieces during English, but he clearly needed it more. "Here," I said, offering it to him. "Maybe this could help."

He graciously took it, opening the pack right there. "My stomach thanks you," he said, taking one Pop-Tart and handing me the other. I tried to decline, but he insisted, saying he wouldn't take the entire thing for himself.

"Mm…" he said as he took a bite. "The s'mores Pop-Tarts are the best."

I nodded in agreement. "My thoughts exactly."

"Smart girl," he mumbled as a piece of crumb flew from his mouth.

My cheeks flushed as I forced myself not to look away and crawl back to my locker. "So, uh…" I said, trying to muster the courage to ask, "got any plans for Friday?"

Oh, god. Why did I ask about Friday? Of course he had plans! He was a cute guy who everyone loved. Probably had a line of girls begging for his attention.

He quirked an eyebrow, a smile pulling at the corners of his lips. "Depends. Are you asking because you want to hang out?"

I could feel my face burn brighter than a tomato. "Um, well, I just thought that I'd ask, you know? But, if you wanted to hang out, I mean, I wouldn't have a problem with it. You know, if you wanted. I'd like to. But only if *you* did."

I sounded like a bumbling moron! *Someone,* please *shut me up this instant.* Not only did I sound stupid, I sounded desperate, which was worse than anything. Especially for my ego, which already hung in the balance.

"I'd like that," he answered, pulling out a notebook from his bag. He ripped off a scrap of paper and scribbled on it, folding it in half before he handed it to me. "I got to run or I'll be late to History, but we'll catch up soon, alright?"

I nodded, trying to hold back the massive grin that threatened to take over. "Alright. I'll talk to you later. And maybe I can teach you about the mysteries of technology," I teased, holding up the paper he'd slipped me. "No one uses paper anymore."

He smirked, shaking his head as he waved, heading off to his class without his water. Hopefully, he wasn't just trying to get away from me, or setting me up like Jack did. But I pushed those thoughts away, filled with too much glee.

How did Mom and Rhi honestly think this feeling could make my powers weaker? I was on top of the world! They must be wrong. They had to be. This felt too good. And I'd prove to them that we didn't need to be social outcasts for the rest of our existence.

I unfolded the note he'd given me:

Text me. I look forward to our date. He ended it with a smiley-face emoji.

He gave me his number. *He gave me his number!*

If I were alone in that hallway, I'd have done a happy dance. It didn't even matter that I was late to English or that I didn't hear the teacher calling my name to answer a question, Wesley had given me his number. He'd called it a date *and* said he looked forward to it.

***

The week rolled by, simultaneously dragging and flying. I was so excited for Friday, it felt like it was taking forever to get there. But by mid-week, as I neared our date, I got nervous, and the time was going too fast for me.

I wanted to look good for Wesley, for him to see me as more than the girl everyone thought I was, and to be treated like any other girl on a date.

So, as soon as school let out, I rushed home to shower, knowing I'd need sufficient time to prepare. I used Rhiannon's shampoo and body wash. It smelled better, more mature. *Mm, violet...* She'd evolved from the scent of warm vanilla and sweet pea you get from the cheap, drugstore sprays. Rhi used *perfume* and smelled more like a woman, which was the goal.

I stepped out of the shower, patting my hair dry delicately, hoping not to frizz it more. Glancing in the steamy mirror, I froze. The edges were tainted with red, an image forming within the steam. The same image I kept seeing: blood. Creatures surrounded by blood. Vampires.

Swiping the image from the mirror, it disappeared.

Not today, Vamps!

Watching a YouTube tutorial, I attempted to apply makeup. I'd practiced each day throughout the week, hoping to be an expert by then. Of course, I was far from an expert, but I didn't do half bad. I'd managed to cover my burn and add a bit of eyeliner, so I considered that a win.

I didn't bother asking Mom or Rhi for help. It would have been greatly appreciated, but I knew they didn't want me hanging out with people and going on dates—and quite frankly, I didn't want to hear them nag. So, I tied my hair in pigtails, braiding it to contain the poof. The colors of my dyed tips braided with my regular ginger color looked kind of… cool. Like streaks of color within the red.

My outfit was cuter than the typical earth tones I wore. But I wanted to dress up for once. I'd decided on a simple red and black plaid dress with black leggings underneath and black ankle boots. Grabbing a black sweater, I slipped it on and glanced in the mirror.

It's like Hot Topic threw up on me. But I looked cute!

Taking a deep breath, I headed downstairs, knowing he'd be here any minute. I rushed to the door, planning to wait outside unnoticed, but the doorbell rang, bringing attention to my scheme.

"Where are you going all dressed up?" Mom asked, skepticism in her eyes.

"I have a date," I blurted out, attempting to run off before Mom began her lecture about how I shouldn't be going on dates.

"Isabel…" Mom said, clicking her tongue in a tsk. "You know that dating will weaken your powers.

With a strong eye roll, I grumbled, "And that's exactly why I didn't tell you."

"I thought it'd be a good idea for her to ask a guy out," Rhiannon answered, coming to my defense. "Might steer any suspicion of Jack away from her if she's dating another guy."

Mom stared for a moment before nodding. "Well, at least let us meet the boy."

I waved dismissively. "Okay, okay, fine! But you guys have to promise to be normal. Don't act all… witchy." I motioned with my fingers to Rhi and Mom.

"We won't. Just open the door before he leaves," Rhi whined, shoving me forward toward the door.

Wesley knocked again and I opened the door, reluctantly inviting him inside. "Come on in," I said, sighing as the words left my mouth. *Great. Please don't let them embarrass me.*

"So this is the Dufort house?" Wesley said, glancing around the room. "Looks mystical." Holding his arms up playfully, he said, "Please don't turn me into a frog."

Mom, Rhi, and I stopped in our tracks, shifting uncomfortably in our positions. Wesley didn't know about Jack or witches, but it struck us with unease, nonetheless.

With a forced smile, Mom said, "Oh, he's funny!"

"Well, I try to be," Wesley said with a shrug, resting his hand on the back of his neck. "Though sometimes, I fail miserably."

Mom chuckled. "Don't we all."

Biscuits stepped in front of me, taking his protective stance. Wesley looked at the cat, squatting down to pet him. "Aww, I love cats. Here, kitty, kitty." He reached out a hand to pet him, but Biscuits swatted and hissed.

"Don't mind him," Mom said. "He's finicky."

Wesley chuckled, standing up again to shake hands with my mother. "Aren't all cats," he joked. "To formally introduce myself, I'm Wesley."

She took his hand, holding it for a moment too long, and I knew she was up to something. Probably using her powers to sense his vibes or some nonsense. But Wesley didn't seem to mind.

His adorably crooked smile had charmed the pants off my mother, and I was a bit more relieved, hoping she would figure that if I was going to defy her wishes, at least it was with a nice boy. One who picked me up at the house, rather than making me wait forever at the dance.

"So… Wesley, is it?" Rhiannon asked, stepping forward. "Where do you two plan to go exactly?" Her hands rested on her hips, and I could only roll my eyes at the absurdity. Even though it was her idea to ask him out, she still drilled him. Even Mom wasn't being so tacky. But without missing a beat, Wesley answered her question with as much charisma as he had when dealing with my mother.

"I was thinking we could go bowling. A few kids from school were talking about going, so I thought it'd be fun."

"Bowling, huh?" Rhi narrowed her eyes, waiting for him to slip up. But he simply nodded and confirmed. "And what time do you think she'll be back, *Wesley?*"

Rhi eyed my mother for help, but Mom simply shook her head and walked up to my sister, literally pulling her away. "That's enough, Rhiannon. Let them get on their way."

I shot her a grateful nod, blowing out a breath of relief, and grabbed my bag that hung on the rack by the door. Wesley tilted his head slightly, his eyes scanning me from top to bottom. My heart fluttered from the intrusion, feeling uneasy with his observing glance, but pleased with the attention.

"You look pretty, Isabel." He smiled, but there was something more in his expression—like he was holding something back. "You look different."

"Oh, it's probably my hair," I answered nervously, holding out a piece of it as proof. As if he couldn't already see it. "It's not as big as usual," I said with a laugh.

Squinting his eyes, he said, "No… it's something else."

"She covered her burn," Rhi blurted, earning a scolding glare from both me and Mom. She shrugged. "What? You *did*."

"Oh, why?" Wesley asked. "Not to impress me, I hope. I think you look beautiful, even with the burn mark."

Rhi stood behind him, her arms crossed as she nodded in approval while my mother stood in awe beside her. She turned to Mom and muttered, "That's what I said, but would she listen to me?"

My cheeks were flaming hot, and if I didn't want to keel over from embarrassment, we needed to get out of there. "*Alright*, I think it's time we headed out." I pushed Wesley through the front door, forcing him to leave before they said anything else to humiliate me. "Love you guys. I'll see you later." I smiled through clenched teeth, Rhiannon winking at me as I left.

She did that on purpose, the little fart!

"It was nice meeting you," Wesley called out to them.

I had been so eager to leave my family, I hadn't thought about the fact that now we were alone, and my confidence wavered between the new Isabel with the dyed hair and cooler clothes and the Isabel that was still a panicked oddball. *Crap*.

Wesley cast me his charming smile, opening my car door. I thanked him, climbing inside. The last and only time I'd been in a boy's car, it ended badly—Him disintegrating in front of me type of bad. Hopefully, tonight would be different.

Hopefully, Wesley really did want to take me out bowling, and it wasn't a lie. Wesley seemed different than the others. Maybe it was because he'd been from another town and hadn't heard all the rumors about my family. Or maybe he was just a nice guy.

"Your house is so cool," he said, admiring the structure before us.

"It's so old," I answered, huffing out a breath. I'd always envied those homes on TV, with the cool built-in shelves and crazy light fixtures.

"Exactly! It's so old and mystical. Reminds me of something you'd see on one of those paranormal shows. But I think that's cool. Everyone else is into these modern homes with the fancy wallpaper, but I think the older homes have more personality and awe."

I cocked my head, seeing my home with a new perspective, as if viewing it for the first time. The paint was peeling and the porch was just a little uneven. The flaws I'd resented suddenly held a new appeal and I wondered how many people had walked across that porch or through that front door.

"I guess it is kind of cool," I said, looking at Wesley, who nodded.

"Definitely cool. My house is so boring. Typical suburban home: white picket fence, rose bushes lining the house. Blech!" He faked a gag, causing me to break out into laughter.

"I don't know much about houses, but I think it sounds lovely."

"Sure, it's lovely. But it matches every other house in the neighborhood. Even the mailboxes are the same. Your house stands out. It might not seem like the perfect house because you're only focused on its beauty in comparison to the other homes. But if you stepped inside, I'll bet it's filled with love and warmth."

Were we still talking about houses?

He pulled out of the driveway, heading down the road toward town, in the opposite direction of the park. At least we weren't heading to the secluded trails.

"You know, Isabel, I've heard what people say about your family," he said.

I sucked in a breath, waiting for him to cancel our date, to declare that maybe the weird girl matched the weird house and he didn't want to be associated with such a strange pair. "Oh?"

"Yeah... People are so dumb, aren't they?"

I snorted, not expecting that answer. "They certainly are. So, it doesn't bother you to be seen with me? Even after hearing such rumors."

"Well, that's all they are, rumors. And after seeing your house, I know that my instinct about you was right."

"Oh? And what is that?"

"That you are everything they claim you to be. Different and strange. Though, I'm not afraid to admit that I think that that's magical. I love that you're not like the others. You stand out. You're unique and I think that's sexy." He cleared his throat, his cheeks flushing red. "Sorry. I mean, I think that's very cool."

I laughed in amusement, ignoring the sexy part. It probably slipped out unintentionally. He couldn't possibly think something like that about *me*. He had to be joking. "You think *I'm* cool?"

"Well, yeah," he answered like it was obvious. "You are."

"Try telling the rest of the school. They'll probably lock you in the insane asylum for saying that."

Wesley and I both laughed, and he shook his head. "They probably would. But let's be honest, now, *they're* the weird ones."

This conversation felt... familiar. It was like the conversations I'd often have with Rhiannon. We would laugh about the other kids, but it was an attempt to make ourselves feel better for standing out. Wesley didn't have that problem. If anything, he was one of the more popular kids, friends with everyone.

"Can I ask you a question?" I asked, curious about his answer.

"Of course." The car was stopped at a stop sign, so he looked over at me.

Under his gaze, it became harder to ask him, but something told me he wouldn't be offended by it.

"Why did you say yes when I asked you out? I mean, you're friends with Rachel and the guys on the team, and they can't stand me. What makes you feel so differently?"

He paused for a moment, his eyes wandering around the car as he thought about the question. Had I worded it correctly? Did I sound like a rambling moron?

"I guess…" he started but stopped, rethinking his words. His eyebrows were furrowed, and I couldn't help wanting to smile at how cute his pensive expression was. But my nerves were all over the place as I awaited his answer.

"I think that everyone has both a beautiful side and a flawed side. Whether they're a Hadley Bat football player, chess player, or whatever. We're all just people, right? We all want to laugh, have fun. To be loved."

His eyes searched mine, holding my gaze. I held my breath as I lost myself in the sea of blue staring back at me, pulling me under the surface, into the suffocating depths. Yet, I wanted to drown in them, to be lost.

"Does that make sense?" he asked, his voice as breathless as I felt—as if it had been stolen from me when I got lost in his blue abyss.

"It does," I whispered, holding onto this moment that was so foreign to me.

A car honked from behind, causing us both to jump. Wesley drove ahead as I stared out the window, wondering what that moment had been.

Connection.

For me, it was chemistry, a spark between us. Something had formed, though I wasn't sure what. Friendship? Love? All I could tell was that we had a moment of understanding, something to bridge the gap—

though I was beginning to realize that maybe the gap between me and everyone else wasn't as big as I'd thought it to be.

We rode in silence for most of the ride until Wesley pointed to a diner and eagerly said, "We should go there after. They have the best milkshakes."

I perked up. "Okay. Are you a vanilla or chocolate kind of guy?"

"Neither. I like strawberry. Or Oreo."

I nodded. "Both admirable flavors, but what about mint or rocky road?"

"Mint, no. Rocky road, yes."

"Well, Wesley, it's clear to me that you have no taste in ice cream if you don't like a mint chocolate chip scoop on your cone."

He shrugged. "And therein lies my flaw. I'm sorry you had to find out this way, Isabel. I hope you don't think any less of me."

I giggled, shaking my head. "No, you're still cool. Still the school heartthrob," I teased.

"Heartthrob, eh? Is that what the girls call me?" He cocked an eyebrow, glancing at me from the corner of his eye.

"Nah, I just wanted to boost your ego a little. Sorry. You can stop puffing your chest out, now."

He chuckled, his laugh smooth like velvet. It was different than his other laugh. More alluring. It sucked me in almost as much as his eyes.

As we pulled up to the bowling alley, a group of kids from school stood out front. "Is that who we're meeting?" I asked, trying to see if I recognized anyone.

"No. Danny invited me, which means Rachel and her plastics are there."

He did not just reference Mean Girls. I'd definitely be mentioning this later, when my confidence wasn't plummeted.

He must've picked up on my shift in energy because, in a calming voice, he said, "We don't have to hang out with them. It can be just the two of us. I'd prefer it, actually."

"No, it's okay," I assured him. "I can't say the same for Rachel, but I'm fine with it. I haven't been bowling in ages, but I'm excited to whoop your butt in there."

"Oh?" he asked with a devious smirk. "You think you can out-bowl the champ?" He pumped his arms in the air, rooting for himself.

"The champ? Hm, maybe I am out of my *league.*"

He let out a hearty laugh, shoving his keys and phone into his pocket. "Nice one." When he got out of the car, he came around to open my door, giving me a hand to help me out. Not that I needed it, but I took his hand, reveling in the touch. His hand was smooth but his fingertips were calloused, and I wondered if that was from playing the guitar. He looked like a guy who would play in a band on the side.

I should've felt more guilty for what happened with Jack, but I didn't. Jack was a monster. And Wesley? Wesley was… kind and genuine. He was cute and sweet. He talked to me like I was a person and not the scum on someone's shoe. With Wesley, I felt somehow worthy of being a normal girl, doing normal things.

He insisted he paid for the shoes and game, despite my pleas of resistance. "If you're really that determined to pay, you can get the next date," he teased. Though, I wondered if he was serious about a second date. So far, we'd had a great time. The conversation flowed smoothly, and there was a moment where I'd completely lost myself in his gaze.

It really did feel like everything I expected a date to feel.

But would it continue to be nice when we saw the others? As we approached them, shoes in hand, I took a deep breath to prepare myself. I was used to their comments but hearing them in front of Wesley would be an added layer of humiliation I wasn't ready to face.

As expected, the girls retained their snooty behavior, making the same rude comments they did in school, though not as many. Amanda seemed the most annoyed by my presence. But Lindsay—she didn't seem bothered. I'd always thought she was the nicest of the bunch, only teasing me when Rachel forced her to.

But because I was there with Wesley, they pretended to be nicer. If you could call it that. Really, they were just holding back on some of their comments, and not saying as much as they usually would. But Amanda's scowl was more than enough to speak volumes.

The guys didn't seem too fazed. They wiggled their eyebrows in the same obnoxious way they would if he'd brought any other girl. In fact, we got along splendidly. With Wesley's presence, I was able to loosen up a bit, keep up with their quips, countering with my own. And they loved it! The guys absolutely loved that I was busting their chops just as hard.

We played a round and—as if by a miracle—I'd actually won. Though, the tingle in my fingers when I held the ball might have had something to do with it. Perhaps, this magic could come in handy after all.

"I guess *the champ* isn't the champ anymore, huh?" I teased, nudging Wes's arm.

He nudged back and said, "That's not fair. I was distracted by your beauty."

Amanda scoffed from behind us, and even without looking at her, I knew her eyes were rolled to the back of her head. But Wesley didn't look away. He stared right at me, ignoring Amanda's bratty behavior.

My face grew warm—not from his gaze, but from the others' presence around us. I just knew we had eyes watching our reactions, and I wasn't ready for them to see my terrible, inexperienced flirting.

"I bet you say that to all the girls," I said, forcing a smile with the joke, though it wasn't heartfelt. I was too focused on everyone else.

"Who wants nachos?" Brad asked.

Wesley turned to face him. "You buying?"

"After that embarrassing defeat, sure." Brad winked as he said, "I need you to annihilate him in round two, Dufort. Can you do that?"

Brad had called me by my last name. Suddenly, I felt like I was on the team or something. "You got it, coach," I answered, giving him a wink back.

The guys *ooh*d around him, and after a few minutes, they returned with three trays of nachos and two of cheesy fries. The other girls looked at the food, picking out a fry or two, but barely touching it otherwise.

Meanwhile, the guys inhaled the food like they were eating for 10. I'd be lying if I said I didn't have a few myself. But it made me laugh when the guys cheered me on, claiming none of the other girls ate like that. The comment made me feel awkward and not the least bit feminine, though I think it was intended as a compliment, judging by the way they said it.

But, hey—nachos were too good to pass up.

Wesley pulled out a few quarters, asking if I'd like to try our luck at the toy gumball machines. I shrugged, taking the quarter and walking with him, enjoying our first minute alone since we'd got there.

"Toy or gumball?"

"Do you even have to ask?" I put my two quarters into the machine, popping open the plastic ball to retrieve my wonderful prize—blue and green feathers. "The standard for toys has changed a lot since I was a kid."

He nodded in agreement, popping open another ball with feathers. Holding it up, he laughed. "What are the chances?"

"What are we supposed to do with feathers?"

He grabbed the feathers and held them behind his back like a tail. *What in the*— Then, he proceeded to dance around, bobbing his head as he strut around me.

I couldn't suppress my cackle as I asked, "What in god's name are you doing?"

"I'm a peacock," he answered, dancing closer to me, nuzzling the side of his head against my shoulder. "What? It works for male peacocks. Now, smile and go run off. I'm supposed to chase you."

I laughed so hard, tears were building in my eyes, and I was begging myself not to unleash the pig-snort laugh in front of him.

He straightened up and swung his arm around my shoulder, pulling me into his side. Though, it was different than when Jack had. I felt comfortable, like the spot at his side was made for me. We headed back to the table where Brad and Danny were asking him what the heck he was doing over there.

"It's my peacock dance," Wesley answered with a shrug, shooting me a smile.

"I'll be right back," I said, heading to the bathroom, shaking my head with laughter because that was all I did around Wesley was laugh. He made me feel… happy. Light. He made me forget who I was and allowed me to be who I wanted to be.

In the bathroom, I touched up my makeup. *Maybe next time I won't cover the scar.* As I stared in the mirror, my eye caught a glimpse of something in the corner.

I turned around, but it wasn't a reflection. It was *in* the mirror. Leaning closer, only inches away, I squinted my eyes and stared harder. The image was a blur, like when the steam from the shower had covered the mirror. Through the haze, I could see the color red.

Blood.

Wesley. Covered in blood, surrounded by vampires who were eating him. Slicing into his flesh and shoveling the blood into their mouths, licking their fingers.

Jesus Christ!

I jumped back, backing up until I hit the stall with my back. The bathroom door opened, and I glanced away for a second to see who it was. But when I looked back at the mirror, the vision was gone, leaving no trace of blood or vampires. Though, the image was burned into my mind.

Still, my heart raced. My mouth was suddenly parched, and I felt exhausted and weak.

"Oh god, it's you," Rachel groaned, narrowing her eyes. It didn't bother me. My mind was worlds away. Her eyes caught the makeup on the sink, and she sneered. "No amount of makeup will take away all that ugly."

"Uh-huh," I answered absently, my eyes glued to the corner of the mirror.

"You know, Wesley doesn't even want to be here with you. He only asked you out because the guys dared him to. It's a pity date." She forced a laugh that was too high-pitched. "He's supposed to be here with Amanda."

So that was why Amanda was extra bitter? She liked Wesley. I *could* believe Rachel—and any other time I would have—but something in my gut told me that her words were lies. That Wesley really did want to be there with me.

But I couldn't focus on that now. I needed to get out of this suffocating room, get home, and beg my mother to do whatever she could to stop these grotesque visions.

Heading for the door, Amanda stepped in front of me, blocking the exit. "If you know what's good for you, you'll stay away from Wesley."

"Yeah, whatever," I said, pushing past her and running out the door. When I reached the table, Wesley saw my panicked expression and came over to my side instantly.

"You okay?" he asked, placing a hand on my shoulder. His eyebrows were pulled in, those blue eyes filled with concern.

"Yeah... No... uh, I need to go home. I'm sorry, but I got a call from my mom, and she needs my help with something urgent. Can we postpone the rest of our date?" *Please say yes.*

"Yeah, absolutely. Let me grab my keys and I'll be right there."

"No, that's okay. You stay, enjoy yourself. I can walk."

"What? No. Let me give you a ride."

"No, please. I insist. It's not that far, and I know a ton of shortcuts. Besides, I can call Rhi for a ride if I need it."

Still, Wesley insisted harder, so I reluctantly gave in to his persistence. As we approached the parking lot, I could hear a weird tune ringing from the shadows near the dumpster. A familiar tune, the same one I'd heard by the window of my room. I clutched my locket, hoping I wouldn't need to use it like I had on Jack.

The ride was mostly silent—nothing like it'd been before. Wesley didn't talk much, though neither did I. All I could think about was the vision. It stuck to my mind like tar, clinging in the most desperate and despicable of ways, tormenting me. I pictured it, over and over—Wesley being torn apart by vampires. Wincing, I forced the image away, bile rising in the back of my throat at the thought.

Wesley dropped me off at home like the gentleman he was, and as soon as he backed out of the driveway, I ran inside to Mom and Rhiannon.

Chapter 5:

Guilt

When I got home, I blurted out my vision, my mouth rambling a mile a minute to get the words out fast enough. My mind was in overdrive, unable to keep up with the thoughts that rapidly passed through my brain. I could barely catch my breath, even as Mom and Rhi led me to the living room, where I sprawled out on the carpet.

Mom and Rhi sat around me, though they chose to sit in the chairs and not on the floor. I explained everything, starting with our date and ending with the vision.

Worried about Wesley, I texted him to apologize for running out and make sure he was okay. But even after 20 minutes, he still hadn't answered.

I glanced at my phone, pacing around the room. "He's not texting back," I said, chewing on my nails. Whipping my phone back out, I scrolled through every social media I had downloaded, looking for Wesley's profile on each one. Scrolling through his posts, I found nothing. But when I looked at other posts that he was tagged in, I saw that he was at a party with Danny and Brad.

At least he's okay.

But dang, I wanted to be with him. Here I was, sitting at home on a Friday night, *again*.

So close. I was so close to finally having what everyone else had, but it was pulled away once more. I wanted to be with them, having fun, laughing and goofing off. Sure, Rachel and Amanda weren't the greatest, but the others seemed to enjoy my company.

"He's probably just busy," Rhi said, peeking over my shoulder at the posts, now that I'd finally stopped moving. "He probably just hasn't seen the text yet and is too distracted by beer pong or something."

"Yeah," I mumbled, hoping that was it. I shoved my phone in my pocket, grabbing at my hair and tugging in frustration. "God, what if he thinks I'm crazy? I mean, the way I took off like that…" I was absolutely mortified.

"The universe might be trying to tell you something," Rhi answered, squeezing my shoulder lightly. "Try meditating."

I waved her away. "You know I'm not into that stuff."

But when Mom suggested I try it, I reconsidered.

"Maybe your ancestors are trying to speak with you, to warn you of something. Take heed of their advice. Follow their guidance. Even when you think it doesn't make sense, listen to them."

For the millionth time, I pulled out my phone and scrolled through social media. "There are new posts," I shouted, a bit more excited than I'd meant, and held out the phone.

"It's a party at Brad's," Rhi answered in a dry tone.

"Should we go there?" I asked in desperation. "Make sure Wesley's okay."

"He looks fine to me," Rhi said, flipping through the pictures and holding out the phone on a picture of Wesley smiling in Brad's kitchen, his arm pumped in the air.

"Yeah, but what if Mom is right and it's a warning for Wesley?" I bit a piece of my nail, spitting it onto the carpet and earning a tsk from my mother. My nails had been chewed down to the fingers, my nervous energy taking root in the stinging from the hangnails I was creating.

Rhiannon sighed, handing back my phone. "Do you even know where Brad lives?" I shrugged. "I think he lives in that gated community on the East side of town. Assuming you could even get past the guards, you have no idea which house it is. What, do you plan to knock on every door until you reach them? Then you'll really be considered the weird girl."

I hated to admit it, but Rhiannon was right. "So, what? We just sit back and wait?"

"I don't see any other option."

Rhi had a way of delivering news with a tough-love mentality. She didn't sugarcoat her statements. That was where my mother came in.

"Honey, I'm sure he's fine. That picture was from only twenty minutes ago. He probably has his phone on silent and hasn't heard your texts and is busy with the party. I know you're worried but relax. I'll make you some tea; we can watch a movie or something to give him some time to respond."

"And if he doesn't?"

"We'll cross that bridge when we come to it. Now, peppermint or lavender?" she asked, heading toward the kitchen with a mug in hand.

"Peppermint."

Rhiannon switched on our old box TV—ancient compared to the sleek, flat screens everyone else had. Her fingers traced over the line of DVDs we had in the entertainment center. Or, should I say, the ugly brown stand that we've had since before I was born. It was probably older than the locket.

"Which movie should we watch?" Rhi asked, holding out a few choices.

My eyes scanned over the options, landing on one in particular that stood out. "*Mean Girls.*"

We'd watched this movie so many times, we could recite the lines. And any other night, we would have. But tonight, my mind was too distracted and unfocused.

Rhiannon nudged me with her arm. "You okay?" Her eyebrows were pulled in with concern. "Glen Coco got four candy cane grams and you didn't even celebrate. Are you still worried about Wesley?"

I nodded, head resting on my knees, my legs pulled up to my chest as I held myself for comfort.

"He still hasn't responded."

"Maybe he passed out or something. Why don't you check his social media again?"

I pulled out my phone, bouncing from one page to the next, looking for Wesley's account. "It's private," I said, confused by the action. "Why? It wasn't private before."

Rhiannon had an expression of pity. I was utterly deflated. He'd changed his status to private, and I wasn't friends with him on there yet. Did he know I was looking at his posts? I hadn't commented or liked anything, so how would he know? Maybe Rachel and Amanda had convinced him to block me, to stay away like the others, and that was why he wasn't answering my texts.

The sting of rejection was a killer. It hurt more than the dull ache of alienation because this time, I really had believed it was more. That Wesley liked *me*.

Hopefully, I would see him Monday and talk to him then.

***

Wesley wasn't at school on Monday. He hadn't answered my texts. He hadn't accepted my friend request. Nothing. It was as if he vanished from my existence.

I sat in English, my first class of the morning, tapping my pencil against my desk. I hadn't paid attention to anything the teacher said about *The Great Gatsby* or the symbolism of the green light. My mind never left thoughts of Wesley. I'd played them repeatedly in my mind, rewinding and rewatching, hoping to find a hint as to what happened, where I went wrong.

Was I overreacting about that vision? Maybe it was a trick of the light.

No. The other visions had been real. Vampires were real. As much as I wanted to pretend they weren't—to pretend my life was normal, that *I* was normal—I couldn't deny it anymore.

Those visions were real, and Wesley was in danger.

Whether he'd chosen to stop talking to me, or if he was being threatened not to, I had no clue. But I did know that the spark I'd felt with him in the car was real, and we had both felt it. I cared about Wesley, and I refused to sit by idly while *who knew what* would happen to him.

So, I did something so uncharacteristically odd of me. I wrote a note to Lindsay. Her social media accounts were set to private, and I didn't have her phone number to text her, so I had to do it the old-fashioned way. A paper note. The thought made me cringe.

Yes, Lindsay was one of the popular girls. The *plastics*, as Wesley had teased. But she was friends with the group at the bowling alley. And she didn't seem as bad as Rachel and Amanda. She was nicer. But most importantly, she sat diagonal to me and might help give me some clarity on this situation. I scribbled:

Hey girl.

No, I couldn't write that. We weren't friends. It would seem too desperate. I erased it and started again.

Lindsay, have you heard from Wesley? I think I left something in his car.

Okay, it was a lie, but I didn't want her to think I was some oblivious girl who couldn't take a hint. If Wesley really was ignoring me, I didn't want to be *that* girl. So, I made up an excuse I hoped was enough to make her help me.

I tapped her discreetly, passing her the note. She opened it, and I waited to see if she would crumple it up, laugh, or just toss it to the side.

But she did none of those things. Her pen glided over the paper, and I eagerly awaited her response.

Without turning, she passed the note back to me, her eyes on the board. I unfolded the note to see curvy, neat handwriting.

I saw him at Brad's party on Friday. He left Saturday morning. That's all I know.

The texting of my mother's age, when people wrote their notes on paper. We continued to pass the note back and forth.

Did he seem mad that I left the bowling alley so abruptly?

She wrote back quickly.

No, but he did seem disappointed. She drew a sad emoji to go with it.

I couldn't help but chuckle to myself before writing back.

I tried texting him, but he hasn't responded. Any advice?

She responded again.

Don't worry about it. The team is prepping for the championship game. He's probably off lifting weights or something. They start prepping early. Are you going??

Lindsay was asking if I was going? Talking like we were friends? Maybe not *friends*, but like we had an acquaintanceship that wasn't filled with hostility and bullying. I leaned in.

I wasn't planning on it. Are you?

She replied again.

Totes! The championship game is the best. The whole town shows up and there's always a big party after. You should come.

Totes? That meant totally, right? For a teenager, my understanding of the current lingo was pathetic. But Lindsay was telling me to come, so that was a plus. Or, maybe she was planning to dump pig's blood on me like *Carrie.*

Why was high school so confusing?

Lindsay glanced back with a smile. A friendly smile, not a sneer. Maybe she *was* being genuine. It touched my heart to know that she would be so kind to me, even though her friends hated my guts. With that in mind, I wrote:

Sounds like fun. Maybe I will come.

So, Lindsay didn't know anything about Wesley. Still, we sent notes back and forth until the bell rang. It was fun to do something an ordinary girl my age does. Something so simple, like passing notes. But it had relieved enough tension to forget about Wesley for a bit.

Until I was on the search for him again after class. But he wasn't there. Wasn't at his locker, in class, or at lunch. Maybe he was absent because he partied too hard and had a two-day hangover? Does that happen to people?

By the end of the day, I'd exhausted my search. My phone dinged and I eagerly swept it from my pocket, hoping for a response from Wesley. But it was… Lindsay? Odd as it was, Lindsay had added me on social media, sending me an official invite to the game.

***

When I got home, I rushed to my mother, telling her about what little information I had: Wesley was at that party until Saturday morning. She laughed when I asked about the two-day hangover, not really answering the question.

"Lindsay did say the team trains a lot starting now for the championship game. Maybe he's busy with training?" she offered, though it didn't ease my mind. Something in my gut told me this wasn't so simple.

"Isn't that still a few weeks away?" Rhiannon asked, popping around the corner and into the kitchen.

Mom laughed, sprinkling some herbs into a cup of tea and handing it to her. "Well, you know how seriously this town takes its sports. There's not much else to do around here."

We sat around the kitchen table, sipping the calming tea my mother had made us. Every day, she'd tried explaining a little more about magic using herbs. Before, I'd tuned it out, uninterested in learning. But now, I wanted to know more about it and had begun to *taste* the magic that she instilled in the tea.

"This has magic, doesn't it?" I asked, holding up the mug.

Mom smiled, nodding as she sipped it. "You can taste it, can't you?"

"Have you always put magic in my tea?" She nodded again and I asked, "Why couldn't I taste it before?"

"You weren't aware."

It dawned on me that the family business might have been more than a simple entrepreneurial side hustle. "The tea that we sell people—the soaps and everything else we make—does that have magic, too?"

My mother had made a business online for selling the homemade products that she makes with herbs and flowers from the garden. Teas, spices, soaps, and other various products. She was a whiz with marketing, and because we weren't marketing to the townspeople who hated us, it was easier for her to make enough profit for it to be her full-time job. Rhiannon and I had helped her with the business for years, completely unaware that the good vibes she was selling held magical properties.

"It does," she confirmed. "I instill the plants with magic as they're growing and use them in the products."

"So, the calming tea really does calm? And the rose petal soap really does bring love?" Dang. I should have used that soap before my date.

"The tea calms and rejuvenates," Mom answered. "It helps us witches to recharge."

I let out a short laugh. "I always thought it was a bunch of hoopla, like crystals and essential oils."

She cast me a knowing expression, her smile filled with warmth and understanding. "Well, the world can surprise you in many ways."

"You got that right," I mumbled, sipping my tea.

"If you're interested in finally honing that magic," my mother said, placing her mug on the table and clapping her hands together, "I have an idea for how we can get some information on Wesley."

My head perked up, and she nodded in response.

"Scrying." She must have noticed my confused expression and elaborated further. "We can enchant the mirror to see Wesley. Our ancestors would use mirrors in rituals of communication with the dead. That is why you always have visions in mirrors or reflections. It's easier to see into the otherworld through the means of an object."

"You think he's dead? That what I saw in the mirror was… true?" I asked, not sure I wanted to hear the answer.

Her face confirmed it, despite her forced smile and kind words. "He is probably training with the team," she lied. But my mother's smile didn't reach her eyes—the classic tell. "It's no guarantee that it will work, but it's worth a shot," she offered with a shrug.

"Let's do it," Rhi said, placing a hand on my shoulder. I nodded in confirmation.

We finished our tea and headed to the basement. My mother pulled out a sage stick to smudge the negative energy from the room and cleanse it. You know, that hoopla that I would've thought was bogus before all this. But now, I viewed it with a new appreciation.

Rhiannon pulled out the candles, arranging them on an altar, which had a wooden symbol in the center. "White and black candles will help with the purity and cleansing of our space. Like the smudge stick, but an added level of protection."

"Protection from what?" I asked. Couldn't we stick some garlic on the front door to keep the vampires away?

"Negative energy," Rhi answered, pulling out two blue candles. "Blue is good for communication and spiritual connection. We use these to promote communication with the spirits."

I took a step back, watching them prepare the space. A weird altar in the center with candles of different colors lit in a line? A smudge stick? Spirits? This was the kind of thing I laughed at. The kind of thing no sane person would believe in. Yet, here I stood, about to communicate with the dead. Or, hopefully not.

Words couldn't even describe the confusion and conflict I felt. But one thing kept me going, pursuing this quest of witchy communication—Wesley. I needed to make sure he was okay. I needed to see him, for only a moment, to put my mind at ease.

He was a good guy. He deserved to be alive and healthy, smiling and laughing.

Mom turned out the lights; the dim lighting from the candles was now the only illumination. With the room dimly lit, it was as if the atmosphere had shifted, almost like the air itself was alive and energized. The air itself was alive and energized but held a thick tension.

My mother took a seat in front of the altar, Rhiannon joining her. I took a deep breath, sitting in the center of them both—directly in front of the weird wooden object with the symbols carved into it. I stared at the object, uneasy with its close proximity.

"Before we begin," Mom said, "I must warn you… If something did happen to Wesley…" she paused, unsure how to phrase it and starting over. "Communication with the dead can be a bit traumatic. Violent deaths transform the soul into something wretched and mean, filled with contempt and cruelty. It turns them into something wicked—dark. If he is *like that*," she said, refusing to say the word, "then it won't be a friendly conversation."

I sighed, preparing myself. "At least we'll know."

She nodded, placing the mirror in front of the wooden object—much to my relief—and began the ritual. She sat in the lotus position, her legs crossed with both feet pulled onto her thighs. Rhiannon and I mimicked the movement.

Humming, she began to chant words that I couldn't interpret, but they had a rhythm, a movement. The words themselves were like a drumroll to a big event.

"Ancestors," she called out in her chant, "please, guide us to the path of truth."

Uneasiness claimed me once more as I stared into the mirror, waiting for something to happen. And like waiting for water to boil, there were no instant results. But I remained patient, allowing my mother to chant and hum, to call upon the ancestors. And after a few minutes, I saw it. A small flicker. A movement.

"Wait," I muttered, holding up my hand as I squinted into the mirror. My mother quieted, but my eyes were glued to the mirror with intensity. "Red. I see red."

Blood.

Seeping down the glass.

"Do you see it?" I whispered. They didn't answer. They simply watched the mirror with me.

I swiped the blood away trying to get a clear visual in the reflection to the image behind the blood.

A locker room. The boy's locker room? A group of vampires circled their prey, tearing them apart, licking up the blood. Was it Wesley? I couldn't tell. I couldn't make out who it was.

One vampire stood apart from the rest who were hunched over the bloody carcass. Without any specific indication, I knew it was the head vampire. Something in my gut told me it was true. He stood over his group, watching them devour this man in the locker room, a pleased expression on his face. But something in that devilish smirk sent a shiver down my spine.

But nothing compared to the fear that had consumed me when he looked up, directly at me, as if he were watching me through the glass.

I jumped back, shoving the mirror away until it hit the floor, losing the vision with it. The candles blew out in sync, shrouding the room in complete darkness. I would scream if I weren't choked for words.

My mother cursed, relighting the candles.

"Did you see it?" I asked. Unable to look away from where that mirror stood, where only the wooden symbol now sat on the altar.

I tried explaining it to them, but they couldn't see what I saw.

"You didn't see the blood?" I asked. "It was dripping down the mirror! I had to smear it away!" My voice rose with each declaration, panic slowly building that even they couldn't see what I could. Even among the witches, I was alienated!

"I saw you rub the mirror, but there was no blood," Rhi answered, a sympathetic look on her face that only made me resent them for not seeing it. She knew I wasn't crazy, yet looked at me with pity.

I grabbed the mirror from the floor, inspecting it. It was just an ordinary mirror. No blood. *I knew what I saw...*

"At least we didn't see Wesley, right?" Rhi tried to make me feel better, but I only felt worse, because I still didn't know if Wesley was okay. Instead, I was given another vision that terrified me to my core. No answers. More questions.

I couldn't get that image out of my head. The way that man looked at me.

He knew I was watching him.

Chapter 6:

Social

Monday morning, I crawled out of bed and headed downstairs to the scent of breakfast wafting through the air. Rhiannon sat at the table, munching on a piece of bacon and a blueberry muffin as she sorted through her binders for class.

Snatching up a piece of her bacon, I popped it in my mouth, pleased with the extra crunch and crispiness.

"Morning, baby," Mom said as she stood over the stove, flipping the final pieces of bacon that sizzled in the pan.

"Morning," I answered with a yawn, stretching my arms.

They were both already dressed for the day, ready to head off to school or work in the garden, while I still wore my fuzzy gamer PJs that had Xbox controllers going all around the legs.

"There are blueberry muffins in the oven," Mom said, sliding a cup of tea in my direction. She quietly scribbled in her notebook as Rhiannon fiddled with her things.

Did no one seriously think all the witchy, ritual stuff was weird? Was no one going to talk about it? We'd just pretend that we were a normal family having a normal breakfast?

I sighed—loudly, I might add—and looked at Mom and Rhi. They glanced up, heads cocked to the side in confusion.

"Is something wrong, Is?" Mom asked.

I shook my head. "Nope. Just wondering why no one's mentioned anything about the ritual from the other night."

It was Monday morning, which meant I'd finally get to see if Wesley would make an appearance at school. Was I nervous? Oh yeah. And I needed a little boost of encouragement to face him. Because if he *was* at school, then that means he'd been avoiding me for a week. But if he *wasn't*, that meant he could be in danger.

Yet, they sipped their tea and nibbled on their muffins like nothing strange had happened.

"What about it?" Mom asked with nonchalance.

I slumped into the chair, resting my head against my hand. It was early and I hadn't fully woken up yet. My nerves were getting the better of me. A part of me didn't want to mention my worry—as if they hadn't heard enough of it over the weekend—but a part of me wanted to talk about it and hear their reassurances.

"Tell me more about the vampires," I said, hoping she'd indulge my request this early in the morning.

"Vampires?" Mom's nose crinkled and her eyebrows creased in confusion.

I nodded. "I think they're responsible for Wesley's disappearance. Maybe if I learn more about them, I can figure this out further."

Past the concern, her eyes lit up, thrilled that I'd finally taken an interest in our family's *lifestyle*. She straightened herself up, clapping her hands together. "What would you like to know?"

"Everything."

"Well, vampires aren't usually in abundance around here. The last time we had a vampire issue, you were a baby. But since then, I haven't seen any lurking around town, aside from a stray here and there."

"Why would they come here?" I asked, trying to piece all this vague information together. "Why come to a small town in the middle of nowhere? Wouldn't they have better luck finding victims in the city, where they can also go undetected?"

Mom shrugged. "I'm not sure, honestly. It's something I've asked myself, as well. Maybe they wanted to start small, in a lower population? Or maybe this location has some special attribute I'm unaware of. Whatever the reason, it seems they're back."

"What do you mean 'back'? What happened when I was a baby?" It'd help to know about the past if I wanted to put this puzzle together. But so many of the pieces were warped, too torn and damaged to see where they belonged. And judging by the expression on Mom's face—the way her eyebrows pulled in, her lips a tight line—I knew she wouldn't answer before she even said it.

"That's a question for another day…"

So, I did what any teenager who wanted to change their parent's mind would do. I begged. "Oh, come on, Mom. I'm finally learning about vampires and now you want to hold back?" I turned to Rhi and whined, "How am I supposed to stop them if I don't know anything about them?"

Ignoring me, she kept skimming through her notes. I nudged her arm and she pulled out the earbuds I didn't know she'd been wearing. "Huh?"

"What do you know about vampires?" I asked, hoping I could get more out of her.

"Not much," she answered, wiping away the crumbs from the muffin she'd finished. "They don't come around often, but when they do, you have one master who will usually recruit others."

"How do they recruit them?"

Rhi shrugged, facing Mom for the answer.

She sighed, her eyebrows raised in defeat. "I don't know exactly how they transition. The master will seek weak-minded humans, recruit them to join, and then change them. The assumption is that they are changed with a bite, but I don't know to what degree they are bitten for transformation or food. Vampires are elusive creatures."

I nodded, soaking in the information. "So, how do you know when they recruit? Do you have some kind of sixth, witchy sense?"

Mom chuckled, shaking her head. "No. But our powers help us to watch over the town to spot them. We listen for anything unusual, any deaths or disappearances. When we hear of one, we do a ritual much like the one we performed the other night, to see if we can find the threat."

"And you guys both do this?" I asked, looking from Mom to Rhi.

They nodded, though Rhi looked less enthusiastic, concern filling her expression.

"Our powers have been dwindling for years," Mom said. "Most of the townsfolk are used to us by now and haven't spread as many rumors in recent years. Fortunately, high school always has an abundance of rumors and ill will. For the last decade or so, I'd use the power fueled by the kids from your school, but when Rhi graduated, that cut out a major source of the ridicule."

"And now I'm the only one left in school," I grumbled, understanding exactly what she was implying. "Does that mean I'm the most powerful?"

Mom chuckled again, clearly amused by my assumptions. "No, honey. You have a ways to go if you want to reach your peak power. But you have great potential and an unlimited source of power. High school is a powder keg of negative energy that can feed us. Because Rhi and I are both out of school and the town mostly ignores us now, we try to channel most of our power into our business, to help others protect themselves from danger."

I sat quietly for a moment, the weight of responsibility suddenly crushing me. "Has it always been like this?" I paused, clicking my tongue against the roof of my mouth. "It's so... stupid. To have to live like this. Did everyone in our family have to do this?"

"Yes."

"But why? Why do we need to be tormented just to help the people who are tormenting us? Doesn't that sound a little..."

"Ironic?" Rhi suggested with a snort.

"That's one word for it. Not the word *I* was going to use, but yeah."

"We were gifted with power," Mom said. "And with great power comes great responsibility."

I rolled my eyes. "Really? You're quoting Spiderman, now?"

She cast me a big grin. "I am. Because it's true. We were granted access to such powers; it's our responsibility to wield them for good. It might not always be an ideal situation, but life rarely is. I understand the bitter resentment that comes with the taunting, but it's part of the balance. Everything in life has balance, and this so happens to be ours."

Why couldn't my responsibilities lie in ordinary things? Homework, school, maybe even a part-time job? But *no*, we had to have *magic*.

"So, it's a family tradition to hunt vampires?" I asked, getting back on track.

Mom nodded. "Yes. My parents were hunters, my grandparents, great-grandparents, and so on."

"What happened to them? Why is the coven just us now?"

She looked away, a strike of pain and conflict showing in her eyes. "Because we're the only ones left. I was an only child and my parents died during a hunt, so I was raised by my grandmother. When I became of age to use my powers, like you, I was confused and defiant. And because I refused to listen to my grandmother, I ended up causing a very bad accident that left our family shunned by the town. It boosted our power unbelievably, but people were hurt in the process. My grandmother used so much power to fix what I'd messed up, she ended up passing only a year later. Which is why I'm so desperate to have you train, so you can use your powers the right way, without harming innocent people."

With that revelation, I couldn't help but feel bad for my mother's experiences. She'd never told me the details of her past, only that her family was no longer around. I'd always wondered but whenever I asked about her family, dad, or dad's family, pain would stretch across her features. It gutted me to see that so I never wanted to push too hard.

"Alright," I said, dropping the subject, again, out of habitual concern for Mom. "When I get home from school, we can train." Hopefully that would lift her spirits.

She smiled and agreed. "You best be getting ready or you'll be late." She shoved a muffin in my hand and sent me up the stairs to get dressed. *Man, I find out I'm a witch and I still have to go to school? Why couldn't I at least go to some cool supernatural school, where I wouldn't be considered a freak?*

When I got to school, Lindsay stood with Rachel and Amanda. She cast me a discreet smile and waved. How unusual to have someone wave at me, but I waved back nonetheless, grabbing my books for English.

I walked to my desk and on it was a folded-up note.

Hey, girl. What's up?

That was all it said. But I could tell by the heart dotting the "i" that it was from Lindsay. Looking behind me to the adjacent desk, she smiled and nodded, reassuring me that it *was* from her.

Just worried about Wesley. I haven't heard from him. I hope he's not hurt.

She took the note from my hand and read the message, her eyebrows creasing as her eyes scanned over the message. With the most serious expression I'd seen on her face, she wrote back:

Don't worry. I'm sure Wesley's fine. He's probably just visiting with his friends back in the city for a bit.

That was one of the rumors. Hopefully it was true, though something in my gut told me otherwise. On a separate line, she wrote:

I added you on Insta and Snap.

Sliding my phone from my pocket, I held it low so the teacher couldn't see as I checked. Sure enough, she did. I accepted the friend requests and slid my phone back into my pocket. As soon as I did, I felt it vibrate.

It was a message from her saying we should message on there now. Then, she asked if I wanted to sit with her at lunch.

Did I? Absolutely. But I was so anxious. Would it be just her or would Rachel and Amanda be there, too? Of course they would; they were her friends. Why would she ditch them to hang out with a loser?

It was everything I'd dreamed of happening. I was finally invited to sit with the cool crowd. But damn, did my nerves eat away at any shred of confidence I'd ever had.

Come lunchtime, Lindsay met me in the hall by the cafeteria and walked me to the table, probably knowing I'd never sit down with them of my own volition. I needed no introduction, as I already knew just about everyone there. We'd sat together at the bowling alley.

And just like before, the guys were more welcoming than the girls. But this time I had Lindsay to watch my back. She told Rachel and Amanda that I was going to sit with them, and if they didn't like it, oh well. Why she was doing so much for me, I had no idea, but I'd take it.

If I'm being honest, lunch with them wasn't as glamorous or entertaining as I thought it'd be. Danny went on for 15 minutes about his car while Rachel and Amanda talked about what color manicure they'd get next. Meanwhile, I quietly ate my pathetic PB&J sandwich, my eyes barely rising above the table. I felt more comfortable with my gaze focused on my sandwich.

When they got onto the topic of the championship game, things livened up. The guys got super pumped and the girls were gawking at their incredibly masculine behavior. To me, it was comical, but I kept my mouth shut and listened, observed. I was finally on the other side of the fence, and before I screwed it up, I had to learn to adapt—to figure out how they behaved—so I could blend in and be a part of their group.

They eagerly started talking about the season—who they thought would play which games or who the coach would likely throw off the team for disobedience or failing grades. But what caught my attention was when someone casually remarked that Wesley wouldn't be there for the championship.

My head popped up and I asked, "Why? Have you heard from him?" I glanced around the table.

Danny shifted awkwardly, forcing a smile. "He missed practice all last week without telling Coach. He'd be lucky to make it back on the team."

"Has anyone heard from him?" I asked again, glancing around the table.

Brad opened his mouth to speak, almost hesitant. "Wes said he needed some space from everything. Don't worry, it's nothing personal. He just wanted to get away for a bit and clear his head from the town. I'm sure you understand."

I did. So many times I would have given anything to get away from this town but still... Something about Wesley just up and leaving, without saying anything, didn't sit well with me. Why would he tell his friends but not his parents or coach? After having such a nice date, why wouldn't he tell me? If he needed space, I would've understood.

It felt like there was more to the story, but I wasn't in the position to demand information or accuse Brad of lying, so I changed the subject, hoping something useful would slip out.

"I had no idea," I feigned ignorance, pretending to believe him. "He seemed so happy at the bowling alley that day."

"Maybe you're just oblivious," Amanda sneered, stabbing her fork into her salad. "Wesley was just being nice around you, that's all."

Lindsay rolled her eyes and turned to me. "Don't listen to Amanda. Wesley was stoked to be on a date with you. None of us knew he was feeling that way." She shot Amanda a scolding look.

"Yeah," Brad agreed. "Wesley had a great time bowling with you. The two of you really had chemistry."

I nodded absently, remembering Wesley strutting like a peacock, which brought a curling smile to the corners of my lips.

The rest of lunch went well. Just like at the bowling alley, we clicked. I fell right into place joking around with the guys, and now that Lindsay was on my side, Rachel was beginning to loosen up a bit, though she still had snarky comments to deliver whenever she could slip them in. Amanda, on the other hand, hated my guts. It was obvious, but I was starting to care less and less about what she thought. She didn't like me. Who cares? That was her problem. The others got along with me well.

They talked about the championship game and the party planned after. "You should come," Lindsay said, whipping out her phone to send me an invite through our socials. And when she did, Brad pulled out his phone to add me. By the end of the day, I had Danny and Rachel added to my social media, too!

How the tides had turned in only a few hours. It was strange, but I didn't question it. I was too thrilled to finally have found a place to fit in.

***

Weeks passed and still no Wesley. No one had heard from him. Though, rumors had spread that he left to move back to the city.

But I didn't believe it. Not in the beginning, anyway.

His parents reported him missing, and his friends had said he often talked about how unhappy he was here, and that he'd mentioned wanting to run away to go back to their old neighborhood. But I knew there was more to the story. I mean, that just didn't sound like the Wesley I'd known. The one who smiled and laughed.

Then again, I had only been out with him one time, so how well did I really know him?

Lindsay was really supportive in my quest to know what happened with Wesley. She asked around the team to see if there was some way to get in contact with him, but they had nothing. Either they didn't know or they weren't saying.

We'd grown closer, texting often. I'd even been added to her group chat with Rachel and Amanda which they'd titled "Hot Bitches." Though I didn't say much on the chat, I was happy to be invited. Slowly, I started to open up more and add more messages to the chat, which led Rachel to start tagging me in posts and sending me funny memes. She'd even liked my posts, no matter how dumb they were. Amanda… not so much.

Mom complained that it was making me weak. "You need to focus," she said for the millionth time as we trained in the garden. I'd been practicing levitation, and flower pots floated inches above the dirt. "Hold it," she said slowly, drawing the words out. "Just a little longer."

My arms grew tired from holding them in the air, forcing out the magic. An alert dinged on my phone, and I glanced down to my pocket, causing the flower pot to slip and fall to the ground, dirt spilling over the edge. *Well, since it fell…* I pulled out my phone to read a message in the group text. Chuckling, I typed back, adding a laughing emoji.

"Focus!" Mom snapped from behind, and I shoved the phone in my pocket. "Now, pick up the dirt, and put it back in the pot."

I stepped forward and bent down but Mom stopped me. "With your magic," she scolded.

Rolling my eyes, I stood up straight, holding out my hands to lift the dirt. My phone dinged again and I pulled it out, one hand still held up, as I texted back.

"Isabel!" Mom scolded. "Put the damn phone away and focus! You're too weak. You need to grow stronger and those kids are holding you back. Now, tell them you'll message them later and turn the phone off."

I grumbled, texting them I'd be back, and slid the phone into my back pocket. Slapping my hands to my sides, I faced Mom.

Her arms were crossed as she stood in her "mom stance," shaking her head in disapproval. "Isabel DuFort, I will not tell you again to put the phone away. I have online orders to complete and I'm putting that aside to train you on your magic. If I don't get those orders out, our ratings will lower and we'll lose customers. Now, I'm not about to risk my business, our *livelihood*, so you can text your friends. You shouldn't be texting them, anyway."

I groaned, grabbing a fistful of my now-straightened hair. "Why does everything have to be about magic? Why can't I just be a normal teenager for once!" My voice rose to the level of screeching. "Focus, focus—that's all you say! Maybe I'm tired of focusing. I just want to hang out with my friends."

"Your friends won't save the town from vampires. You need to train so you can take on your responsibility as a witch. It's time to lose the immaturity and grow up. You can't always have things your way."

My eyes narrowed, though I didn't speak. I crossed my arms to match hers, glaring at my mother. "Well, can't we at least go back to the visions? I'd rather train with that."

"It doesn't work that way." I could hear her voice growing in frustration. She was reaching the edge of her calm. One more push and she might blow. "You can't control your visions. The only thing you can do is strengthen your magic!"

Rhi stepped outside, her face and hands covered in clay, smears on the front of her smock. "What's going on? What's with all the shouting?"

"Mom won't leave me alone about this stupid magic," I yelled, flopping into the chair outside the garden.

Rhi hunched down in front of me at eye level. "I know magic can be frustrating, Is. But tell you what, if you put the phone away for a bit, I'll help you learn how to make a plant sprout." She raised her eyebrows, giving me a soft smile. "What do you say? Want to try it?"

I took a deep breath, taking a minute to think it over. Honestly, I was making them wait to be dramatic. I didn't want to give in too easily. "Okay," I finally answered, turning my phone off so it wouldn't vibrate anymore.

Though the distraction remained. Throughout the rest of training, I kept thinking about that last message I didn't get to read.

Chapter 7:

Hate

Because no one had heard from Wesley for nearly a month, we'd tried a few more communication rituals—séances—but each time, we came up empty. I had even convinced Rhiannon to come with me to the bowling alley after they closed to do a séance there. We'd used my enchantment magic—something I started practicing daily, thanks to my mother's insistence—to unlock the door and slip right in. But even that produced no results.

Without any proof of ill intentions, I had nothing to go off of, just a growing concern something bad happened to him. I had nothing to prove that, though. Maybe he really had tired of this small town and left.

So, after weeks, despite my strong conviction that something was wrong, I had no choice but to just give in and believe the rumors. To stop tormenting myself with the possibility that something was wrong. I had to face the truth: Wesley just didn't want to stick around such a small town.

He didn't want to stick around me.

During this time, I'd grown even closer to Lindsay. We talked constantly between classes and on our social DMs. She began mentioning me in her posts and liking things that I reposted. She wanted to help me with my image, which I was super grateful for. I didn't actually talk to those people, but if they wanted to be my friend online, I sure as heck wasn't about to turn them down.

It was always a bit awkward being around Amanda or Rachel alone, even with our Hot Bitches group chat. Face-to-face interaction was always different. But after the first few times, we'd gotten past it and learned how to talk without insults. Or, not many of them.

If you had told me a month ago that I would be hanging out with the popular crowd, there is no way I would have believed it. Yet, here I was.

So, I continued to hang around Lindsay and the others to get my mind off Wesley. Mom and Rhiannon warned me that this new "lifestyle," as they had put it, would lead to trouble. That it was sucking my powers, making me weak. But I waved off the paranoia, thinking nothing of it.

Besides, that vision ruined my date with Wesley, and I hadn't heard from him since. I left him at that bowling alley for what? A bad feeling? Obviously, nothing had come from it, so why bother? If Wesley was dead, we would have communicated with him by now, right?

So, when I had more visions, I just ignored them and pushed them away. They weren't doing anything for me anyway. Those visions were nothing but a headache.

Honestly, I was happy. For once in my life, I felt like a normal kid at school. I finally found my place. And my family wanted me to give it up? After all those years of seclusion and torment, they wanted me to just crawl back into the shadows, forever the outcast?

No, thank you.

Their insistence made me resentful. I loved them, but they were plucking every last one of my nerves, like strings on a violin. Why couldn't they just leave me alone and be happy that I'd finally found my place in the world? Rhiannon knew more than anyone how much this meant to me, yet she still wanted me to leave it. I think it was her reaction that hurt the most.

Their reluctance at my new *lifestyle* was irritating. My irritation had resulted in me snapping at my mother often, arguing during my enchantment training more so than I'd argued with her before. Every time I dropped an object or couldn't do something perfectly, she would blame my lifestyle and weak powers.

But if she would just listen to me...

I know, she's my mom and only wants what is best for me, but who is she to decide? It's my life, so shouldn't I be the one to get that choice? Wouldn't I know more than anyone what was best for me?

And if I heard either of them mutter something about my teenage hormones one more time... let's just say those hormones would go berserk.

All I'd ever really wanted was to have friends. I couldn't care less about magic.

Although, I must admit that having the powers of enchantment did have its perks. Like, enchanting my pen to do my homework when my hand was tired. Or to turn off the light switch when I didn't feel like getting up. Sneaking into the bowling alley to do that séance with Rhi. Yeah, magic was alright then.

But fighting vampires? No, thank you. If I was honest with myself, I was scared to have another run-in like the one I had with Jack.

Today, I sat in my English class, passing notes with Lindsay. Her friendship felt truly genuine. Our conversations weren't filled with fake compliments like with the others. Really, she had so much potential if she'd just drop Rachel and Amanda. But she lacked the confidence. In her mind, she needed Rachel to be cool. If only she could see how much she stood out, in a good way, on her own.

Lindsay was a good person. She just needed to lose her insecurities. Stop trying so hard to be cool because she was cool on her own. Like the note she'd passed that morning:

OMG, have you seen Heather's outfit? Can you believe she wore that shirt!

Lindsay was so much better than that snobbish behavior, and I'd help her see it.

I know, right? She's rocking that shirt. So cute!

I liked Heather. Making fun of her didn't feel right. When I passed the note back, Lindsay paused for a moment before writing back. Suddenly,

I was worried that Lindsay was mad that I didn't respond the way she anticipated. Would she drop me now? Think I'm no longer cool or fun?

I peeled open her note.

You're right! So cute!

It felt good to stop the bullying, even if it was just one comment. But it was one less comment of negativity floating through space. That was me, Isabel Dufort, changing one bully at a time.

At lunch, I sat with Lindsay and her friends, chatting and laughing. No more sitting alone, counting the minutes that ticked by until my next class. No more sneaking my lunch to an empty room, just to hide from any bullying or torment.

Things were going well until one day after school when I was walking home with Lindsay. When I shoved my foot so far in my mouth, there was no getting past it…

We'd made it a habit of walking home together each day. Lindsay didn't live far and neither of us liked to take the bus.

Just after leaving the school, Danny pulled up with Rachel in the passenger's seat. The two of them were going out, so riding home together was typical. Amanda and Brad sat in the backseat, his arm around her shoulder. As far as I knew, those two were friends, though Amanda often made goo-goo eyes when she stared in Brad's direction.

"Get in," Danny called out, parking beside us.

Lindsay climbed into the backseat, telling the others to scoot over to make room for me. Amanda scoffed, shoving her things to the side, sitting on Brad's lap as I climbed in, taking the window seat.

"Want to go to the mall?" Lindsay asked everyone in the car.

"Sorry guys, I can't hang today," I answered, already dreading the response. I didn't want to go home, but I'd ignored too many after-school training sessions with Mom for her to let me go.

"Oh, come on!" Lindsay begged. "Come to the mall with us."

Rachel groaned. "I'm tired of the mall. Half the stores are closed down anyway. Let's go to the shops on Fifth."

"We can bring you home right after," Brad suggested, his eyebrows raised. Amanda shifted on his lap, turning away from me, and blocking my view of him in the process.

I shook my head. "Sorry. No can do. Mom said I need to be home after school today."

Lindsay mumbled, "That sucks," as Danny drove toward my house.

The atmosphere had tensed from my rejection, and I worried they might think I was lame and not want to hang out with me as much, so I added, "Well, I guess a few minutes won't hurt..."

Brad reached across the backseat and patted my shoulder, shouting, "Yeah! Let's go to the arcade!" Which earned another groan from Rachel—and a look of annoyance from Amanda.

We went to the arcade, grabbing a few snacks before loading our cards with coins for the games. I was a bit short on money, but Lindsay covered me. She was always the most gracious of the bunch.

My phone buzzed and I looked to see my mother's face on the screen. *Nope.* Not now. I ignored the call, shoving the phone back in my pocket—doing the same every time she called.

After a while, I headed to the bathroom to touch up my makeup. I'd gotten better at applying it, and you could barely tell I had a scar. As I touched up my mascara, I saw the mirror tainted red at the corners but ignored it. I applied my lip gloss and headed back out.

See? Life was easier when I ignored the visions.

When I got back to the table, Brad motioned for me to sit next to him. Not wanting to be rude, I accepted, though I could see the glare in Amanda's expression by the way her lips were pulled tight into a straight line and the resentment in her eyes.

Brad had his arm around her in the car, and though they weren't dating, she probably had a big ol' crush on the guy. And here he was, inviting me to sit next to him.

He had his arm around my chair, not on my shoulder, but closer than I'd have wished him to be. Why was Brad being so friendly all of a sudden? Did he like me or something? I had zero interest in him like that and didn't want him to get the wrong impression.

"So, Isabel," he said, leaning toward my chair. "Got any plans for the weekend?"

Amanda's eyes narrowed into slits, watching our encounter like a hawk waiting to dive in and attack the field mouse.

"Nothing in particular," I answered, trying to be polite but not seem interested. "I'll probably hang out with Rhiannon, watch some movies or something."

"Oh, yeah? Well, let me know if you'd like some company," he said, shooting me a wink.

Amanda was fuming. I swore; steam could shoot out from her ears like in a cartoon. It was almost comical to watch.

Personally, I couldn't stand Amanda. Sure, Rachel was the leader of the group, and her comments far exceeded anyone's, but Amanda was sneaky. Petty. At least Rachel was blunt. If she didn't like something, she'd tell you. There was never a question of where you stood with her. But Amanda? She would plot against someone, working in underhanded ways to take them down, which disturbed me more than any amount of bullying from Rachel.

"Rhiannon Dufort?" Danny chimed in. "Man, she was hot."

That time, I was with the girls when their eyes rolled, though I figured Rhi would get a kick out of that later.

"You know what isn't hot?" Amanda spoke loudly over the others to be heard, silencing the group. "That comment Isabel made about Lindsay's outfit the other day." She turned to me, adding loudly, "What was it you said? That she looked fat and slutty?" Her lips curled into a devious sneer, triumph evident on her face.

Lindsay gasped, her mouth gaping open from shock. "You said that?" Her tone was a mix of anger and hurt—rightfully so. I never meant to hurt her. And yeah, maybe I did say something along those lines, but it wasn't intended the way it was taken and definitely wasn't intended for Lindsay's ears.

"I didn't say it like that," I said in an attempt to defend myself. "I said your curves were showing. I just meant that you don't usually wear that kind of outfit, and I didn't want people getting the wrong idea about you. It was taken out of context."

"The wrong idea? And what kind of idea is that?" Lindsay snapped, her voice growing in irritation. "That I'm a slut? That I'm so fat, my hips poke out of my shirt?"

The table fell silent, each person watching like they had popcorn as the scene unfolded. No one spoke. It was so quiet, you could hear a pin drop. Well, aside from the music that played over the speakers, and the constant buzzing and dinging of different arcade machines. But in that moment, I couldn't hear any of those things. I could only hear my heart pounding in my chest, hoping I could get Lindsay to understand that I wasn't calling her those things and Amanda was skewing my words.

"No, Lindsay! You're gorgeous!" I answered with insistence. "And you're a great person. I didn't want people to think otherwise based on your outfit," I answered, realizing the instant it left my mouth that it was the exact *wrong* thing to say.

Lindsay shook her head, eyes sparkinging with a poisonous glower. "Yeah, but a *true* friend wouldn't talk about my outfit behind my back. She'd come tell me to my face!"

"I wasn't trying to badmouth you or anything. It's been taken completely out of context. You're getting way too upset about nothing." My defense had gotten me nowhere. The girls all stared at me with their judgmental expressions.

Isn't that the pot calling the kettle black? They've badmouthed me for years, and she was getting upset about something that wasn't even as big a deal as she was making it out to be? What a hypocrite!

"Besides," I said, narrowing my eyes to match theirs. "You're one to talk. Didn't you say Amanda's new shirt looked ugly?"

The situation was already tense—both of us now standing, our fists balled at our sides, hands flying everywhere—but the last thing we needed was for the guys to *ohh* behind us, heating up the argument to the point of Vesuvius.

Lindsay planted her hands on her hips, staring hard. I nearly folded under her glare, but she turned and stomped off, leaving the table without another word.

I ran after her, catching her by the door. But she refused to stop and pushed past me, storming to the parking lot. Her ride was inside—was she planning on waiting in the car or walking home?

"Lindsay, wait!" I called out, finally catching up to her again. "Lindsay, please, can we just talk about this?"

She halted her step, swiftly turning on her heels to face me. "Alright, Isabel," she said, her voice high-pitched and bitter. "You want to talk? I'll start." She threw her hands down, sighing as she looked away. Bringing her gaze back to mine, her voice was softer, though still resentful. "When did you become the mean girl? Talking about your friends behind their backs? That's not like you, and honestly, I don't want to be friends with someone like that."

"Are you kidding me!" My voice rose with every word. I'd followed her with the intention to patch up this mess, but she wanted to act like that? "You're friends with Rachel and Amanda, and they're *way* worse than I am!"

She shook her head, tipping it back, as if looking to the sky for answers. "You're different. You're not like them, which was why I held you to a different standard. But you keep acting like this and you'll be just like them. A little Rachel replica." She faced me again, her cheeks burning a bright red that resembled a tomato. Lindsay was really worked up, so angry her face had grown hot. "Do you want that? To be mean like her? To make fun of others?"

"What are you talking about? What am I acting like? All I said was that your curves were showing. Amanda's the one that changed it to slutty. But go on," I motioned with my hands, waving her away, "go back in there and hang out with your *friends*."

"Screw you," she spat, walking away. Not toward the car, to me, or to the arcade. She walked in the opposite direction, and in that moment I didn't care to follow her.

"Whatever," I shouted, throwing my hands up. "Forget you, too!"

I stomped off toward the arcade, debating asking Danny for a ride home. But I could see through the doors that the girls were obviously angry with me, and I didn't bother going in. Instead, I called Rhiannon for a ride.

Waiting on the curb outside, I replayed the scene in my head. All this because stupid Amanda was jealous about Brad showing interest in me? It wasn't my fault that he liked me! And now Lindsay was mad and not talking to me. Which sucked because Lindsay was the one person I actually liked.

Amanda: one.

Isabel: zero.

You happy now, Amanda? You won! Everyone hates me again thanks to you.

I'd be lying if I said that there wasn't a part of me that was angry with myself. Because I knew that I'd done something bad. I talked about Lindsay behind her back. No, I hadn't intended it the way Amanda meant, but I should have known better than to say anything.

But damn them both for making me feel like this! I was finally happy, and they'd taken that away in an instant. All because Amanda was a jerk and Lindsay wouldn't listen to me.

All this conflict gave me a headache.

Rhiannon pulled up to the arcade, and I slid into the front seat. "What's wrong?" she asked, hearing only a sliver of the story until now.

I explained the entire situation on the ride home, griping about how annoying it was and how angry I'd been.

"Can you believe her?" I scoffed, rolling my eyes. "She said I was like Rachel. Me!"

But when Rhiannon didn't take my side, it stung.

"You know," she said, peeking at me from the corner of her eyes as she turned onto our road, "I used to be the same way. Remember my popular days in school?"

How could I forget it? A few years ago, Rhiannon was dating, going out with friends, doing everything I was doing now, only she was the queen and not the worker bee.

"This might sound like a cheesy after-school special, but just listen to me before you judge, okay?" Without waiting for confirmation, she continued. "I wanted so badly to be cool like the other kids. And when I found out about our powers, I took the same path you did. I realized that all those years of isolation were because of some stupid magic! Who would want that? I'd rather have friends or boyfriends, rather than be some magical nobody in an old house, manipulating people through magic."

I nodded, understanding the sentiment. No judgment here.

"And like you, I started treating my friends like trash for the sake of looking cool. The power of popularity had changed me, and I made the same mistakes you are now. I became sneaky and deceitful, doing whatever it took to stay at the top."

Okay, now I was judging. Not her actions, but her reason for telling me this because I knew what was to follow. She was going to tell me I'm changing and should go back to being a nothing—wasn't it just earlier today I had *stopped* the bullying!

Crossing my arms, I slid down in the seat, staring out the window. "Why are you telling me this?" My tone was sharp. Filled with irritation.

"Because, Isa! I don't want you to make the same mistakes I did. I *deeply* regret my actions. The things I did to the people who treated me well... it was messed up. All that manipulating and lying, it turned me into someone I never want to be again. I'm just trying to help you, give you a heads up before you shoot yourself in the foot."

"Well, I'm not like you and I can handle myself, thanks."

I could see Rhiannon's reaction through the reflection in the window. The disappointment in her eyes, accompanied by a tsk. Maybe I'd been a little too harsh. She opened up to me and I shot her down. But how was this not manipulation right now? Wasn't she only trying to get me to quit being friends with them by making me feel bad?

"Fine. Do what you want," she answered. "But I will tell you that once I gave up that popularity and embraced my power, I felt a million times happier. The tension lifted and I no longer felt the need to prove myself."

We had pulled into the driveway and were sitting in the parked car. I looked at Rhi, shaking my head.

"I don't understand why you're so dead set on me fighting vampires," I said, not as angry as before, but still annoyed enough to make it obvious in my tone. "I'm finally happy. I have friends. Why does everything have to be about magic? If being alone is how it is, then I don't want the stupid magic!"

I flew out of the car, slamming the door behind me and running into the house, to my room.

Why couldn't everyone just leave me alone! All these expectations... Lindsay holding me to *higher standards*, Rhiannon insisting I revert back to the caterpillar when I've already transformed into a butterfly, my mother dying to teach me magic to inherit the family trade.

It was all too much.

I sat on the edge of my bed, rocking back and forth with my head in my hands. *It was all too much!*

A weird energy emitted from the locket, like a buzzing around my neck and on my chest where it sat. *Not now!*

I pulled off the locket, gripping it in my palm. The radiating energy numbed my hand, making it zing like it'd been asleep.

Everything in my life had crumbled in a single day—a single hour—and it wanted to act up now? *Why couldn't magic just leave me alone?*

"What do you want from me?" I yelled, throwing the locket into the wastebasket across the room.

Peeking through the wicker of the wastebasket were rays of golden light, illuminated from the locket. The glow from the locket shone against the mirror above it, casting a blinding light that bounced through the room, from one reflective surface to the next.

And in the haze of light, I could see something in the mirror. No, not some*thing*, but some*one*.

"No!" I screamed, jumping from the bed to the mirror. I pointed my finger, pushing against it like it were an animated person, living and breathing before me. "Enough with the visions! I don't want them! I don't want vampires!"

The locket ignored my requests, glowing brighter. Bright enough that the entire room was enveloped in light, until the only thing I could see was the vision in the mirror.

Forced to face away from the blinding light, I looked into the mirror.

The vision was different.

It was Wesley. Smiling. Laughing. He was walking with the team, joking and shoving teammates playfully.

My heart filled with warmth at the image… and a pang of hurt from his abandonment.

Why did you leave me, Wesley? You were the only one who didn't force a bunch of expectations on me. The only one who allowed me to truly be myself.

Why did you go?

He looked at the mirror, his smile plastered on his face, the image frozen in time like a photograph.

Great, the mirror was taunting my heartbreak. Reminding me of what could have been and shoving it in my face that it was gone.

The image came to life once more and Wesley waved goodbye, his smile filled with sadness as he turned and walked away, shrinking in size.

Thanks for that, mirror. That made me feel freaking fantastic. Ugh!

Now I felt the weight of loss and concern all over again.

But a new image appeared. One with the vampires eating someone. *No, no, no! Not this again.* I looked away, afraid of the image. But when I looked back, the vampires had disappeared, and the bloody corpse was all that remained.

Wesley!

It was his corpse. His bloodied body, lying motionless and torn apart, ravaged by vampires.

I screamed his name, touching the mirror, but as I did, everything faded. The light around me disappeared. The mirror was nothing more than glass.

My chest heaved up and down, gasping for the air that had been knocked out of me with that vision. Backing up, I landed on the bed, sitting there for a minute to decipher what had happened.

I'd tried ignoring the visions, but the locket had *forced* me to see it. And in that moment, I was certain that my original convictions were correct.

Something *had* happened to Wesley. Deep in my gut, I knew it to be true.

Wesley was dead.

He was dead.

Tears pricked at my eyes, and I tried to rapidly blink them away, but they were persistent, flowing over my cheeks. A small whimper turned into a heavy, unending sob.

The next thing I knew, I'd spent two days crying over Wesley's death. Mom and Rhi checked on me, but I ignored their pleas to get up. I turned away, tucked myself further into my pillows, and cried some more.

It was my fault he was gone. I should've taken those visions more seriously, but I didn't. And now...

I let this happen. I should've taken action.

That was when it dawned on me—sitting around moping would do no good. It wouldn't bring Wesley back and it wouldn't stop this from happening to someone else.

I stood from the bed and grabbed the locket from the wastebasket, holding it in my palm. The energy from earlier had receded.

"Okay," I said, holding it up. "I'm listening now."

Chapter 8:

Taunt

I stood at my locker on Monday morning, the atmosphere grim. Not only from my own personal transgressions but because over the weekend, a student had gone missing.

Students were being called into the administrator's office to speak about any information they may have about the student.

First, Wesley. Now, this kid?

Something was happening in this town, and I was stupid for ever denying it. For putting my own selfish desires above all else. The locket made me realize this. By forcing me to see that vision, it showed me the severity of my actions, and I knew it needed rectification.

Grabbing my books, I shoved them into my backpack and headed for the bathroom. While in the stall, a group of girls walked in, talking about the missing kid.

"Of course he ran away," one said. "Who wouldn't want to get away from this crap-hole town?"

The other scoffed. "Oh, come on. He was the star of the basketball team. Why *wouldn't* he stay?"

I peeked through the slit in the stall, watching as they applied makeup and primped their hair.

"Who cares?" the first girl said, puckering her lips and popping them. "Basketball isn't that great anyway."

"Well, you gotta admit it's odd. I mean, that's the third person since last week to go missing."

"Third? I thought Wesley was the only other one. And everyone knows he left for the city. His parents need to get real and face the facts—their son left. Stop searching for someone who's not even missing."

I wanted to smack that girl upside her head for her naivety. Then again, that was me a few days ago.

"Yeah, but did you know that Sarah and John are also missing?" The other one said, catching my interest.

"Then why haven't we heard about it?" she asked, crossing her arms.

"Because Sarah's mom is a drunk, and John's father hasn't been home since last month. No one gives a crap about them. Probably doesn't even know their kids are gone."

No one gave a crap, she said. No one cared. *I needed a loser.* Jack's words came back to me. The exact criteria for a vampire's victim.

***

A week later, those girls returned to the bathroom to discuss a new missing teen from our school. And just like before, I was in there when it happened. Though, this time I was standing at the sink washing my hands.

"Can you believe it? Now Dylan is gone," the second girl said, pursing her lips for the mirror and winking comically at herself.

The other girl rolled her eyes. "No way. I just saw him last night."

"Yeah, but he was looking pretty rough, wasn't he? Pale and sick looking."

She nodded in agreement.

"Yeah, because he'd just finished taking a bunch of shots," the other scoffed. "People are just overreacting. Kids are finally realizing how boring this town is, and they're leaving. I mean, think about it. Half those kids are almost eighteen, so they're basically adults, anyway."

"Then wouldn't it make sense for them to all run away together?" I asked, forcing myself into the conversation. "Or leave a note or something?"

"Oh, didn't you hear?" The second girl asked. "He sent a text to his parents saying he was fine, and just needed a break."

My eyebrows creased in skepticism. "What if someone else sent that text, pretending to be him?"

The girls laughed, shaking their heads. "You watch too many crime shows," one teased as they left the bathroom.

After learning that information, I needed to talk to Mom and Rhi. There was an idea I'd been toying with, but I needed help sorting out the details. Not even bothering to wait until the end of school, I skipped my final period to head home early.

When I got home, I told Mom about the missing boy, suggesting we do another ritual.

"We should wait for Rhiannon to get home," she said, fixing us a cup of tea as we waited. "That way we can have more power."

I nodded, taking a slow sip.

"But while we wait, maybe we should discuss you leaving school early." Her lips were pursed, eyebrows raised in annoyance.

After Rhi finally got home—and ended her lecture about a good education and staying in school—we finally sat down to do another ritual.

"Actually, I have another idea," I said, taking a seat beside her and Rhi in front of the altar. "You said enchantment is based on the user's ability, and is strengthened when paired with the right object?"

Mom nodded, her eyebrows creased in suspicion. "The enchantment is stronger when it reflects the purpose of the object." I'll bet she was wondering, *just what does my daughter have in mind?*

"And when we are scrying, having a séance—whatever you want to call it—we're enchanting the mirror to show us, right? And it's stronger with a mirror because we're trying to *see* something?" Again, she nodded. "Well, if we're trying to communicate, what if we enchanted the phone and called him?"

Rhiannon's head perked up, eyebrows raised in curiosity. I think even she'd prefer that over a dingy old mirror.

"Hmm…" My mother tapped her finger to her chin, eyes looking up as she considered the thought. "I mean, theoretically speaking, a phone *can* be enchanted. I don't see why it wouldn't work. Though, I'm not sure if the technology aspect would interfere with the magic."

"It could boost it," Rhiannon offered with a shrug. Mom's head cocked to the side, interested in the suggestion. "Think about it, magic is the manipulation of energy. Technology uses electromagnetic energy. You could manipulate electromagnetic energy. Isn't that what ghosts do on those ghost-hunting shows?"

Mom's expression remained skeptical, though Rhiannon and I were bursting with excitement. Could I have just found a new way of using our magic? A new-age form of enchantment?

Discarding the mirror to the side, Rhiannon brought down one of her old cell phones to use as a conduit and placed the phone on the altar, taking a seat beside me.

Mom joined at her side, and we began our chanting—Rhi and I were experts by now, given how many attempts we'd made in this past month. My eyes closed, giving me the concentration to focus my mind on enchantment.

My body buzzed, as if the energy was flowing through me. Though after a moment, it silenced. Peeling my eyes open slowly, I looked at the phone. An image had materialized, slowly growing in clarity.

A… person? Man?

Wesley!

It was Wesley.

After a month of uncertainty—a month of nothing—Wesley appeared on the screen.

I snatched the phone, holding it close to my face as I looked at it. Relief flooded me to see him, to finally reach him, until it hit me…

He was dead.

This was his ghost on the phone. And just as Mom had warned me weeks before, he was filled with rage.

"Isabel Dufort," he said with spite.

I dropped the phone, shocked by his tone. My mother picked it up and placed it on the altar so we could all see him, though his focus was only on me.

"Jesus Christ, of all the useless people to rely on, I got stuck with you. No wonder everyone thinks you're such a loser. You had all the power in the goddamn world, and couldn't even save me? I gave you the time of day when no one else would, and you repay me with this bullshit? Like I said, fucking useless."

His words cut through me like a knife, the wound as tangible and real. I winced, turning away. I couldn't face him. Couldn't face the truth: that he was right. I could have saved him, and I didn't.

"You turned your back on me!" he screamed, his voice echoing through the basement. "What kind of a bitch would do that?"

"I'm sorry!" I cried out, holding back the tears that were seconds from pouring down my cheeks. "You're right, Wesley. I should have saved you, and I didn't. I'm so, *so* sorry."

He chuckled, his deep laugh more menacing than humorous. Nothing like the laugh he'd graced upon me before. This was dark. It held malice. "*You're* sorry? You? *I'm* the one stuck in this hell!"

"You're right!" I choked on the words, swallowing past the hard lump in my throat. "I'll fix it, Wesley. I should have taken it more seriously, but I'll do whatever it takes to fix it, to get you back."

"Are you an idiot?" he sneered, eyes narrowed into slits. "It's too late! You're the reason I'm dead!"

"Please," I begged, my voice cracking from the high pitch. "I'll do anything to make it right. I don't know how, but I will. Even if it means sacrificing myself. I'll find a way."

A devilish smile crept at the corner of his lips, a darkness in his eyes. Those once blue eyes that I'd have given anything to drown in were now pulling me into their depths. Their dark depths, full of animosity and despair, nearly black and not the gorgeous blue they'd been before.

"That works for me," he answered, his hand coming toward the screen. No—*through* the screen! His mist-like arm emerged from the phone, too vaporous and surreal to make contact. Or so I assumed, but he grabbed me, as tangible as anyone else.

His fingers wrapped around my neck, gripping tighter than I knew possible. "Fucking bitch," he grunted, trying to pull me toward him.

Mom shouted something I didn't understand, dissolving the vaporous arm, and she grabbed the phone to end the call, sending Wesley back to his ghost realm.

I collapsed on the floor, coughing and gasping for air. Rhi's arm ran along my back to comfort me, as Mom told me it would be alright in a soothing tone. But all I could do was sob as I choked on air and phlegm, utterly distraught by Wesley's accusations.

Because I knew they were all true.

"It's alright," my mother cooed, her arm on one side, Rhiannon's on the other.

I shook them both off, backing away. "How!" I shouted. "How could it possibly be alright? It's my fault he's dead. I should've taken the visions seriously. I should've listened!"

That conversation had broken me. Everything I'd wanted, the thought of giving up my new lifestyle, was nothing but selfish naivety. How could I have been so stupid? Wesley was dead because of me. "It's all my fault," I muttered, grabbing my legs and pulling them to my chest, sobbing into my knees. "It's my fault."

"Isabel, listen to me," my mother said, crouching down in front of me, tipping my head up with her finger. "It's not your fault. You didn't kill Wesley. You didn't do anything wrong."

How could she be so blind? Could she not put aside the fact that I'm her daughter and see me for the monster I was?

"It *was* my fault!" I shrieked, choked by the spit from my crying. I coughed so hard that my lungs hurt. My throat hurt. *I* hurt.

"It isn't about what you did or didn't do," Mom said, her tone stern. "What matters is what you do now. We all make mistakes. What counts is how we handle them. Do you learn from them or repeat them?"

Rhiannon came up to my side again, her hand on my arm. "Mom is right. What's done is done. Wesley is gone. So, do you sit here and cry about what you *didn't* do, or are you going to do something now? Do you want to help Wesley?"

I nodded, my vision blurred from tears, my face dripping with too many tears and snot to swipe away with my sleeve.

"What do I do?" I asked, my voice hoarse and weak.

"We train."

I tried to stand but stumbled over my feet, grabbing their arms for support. "I don't think I can do anything. I feel like I'm going to pass out."

"That's because your powers are weak," Mom answered in a tone that didn't necessarily say *I told you so,* but it was enough to earn an eye roll. "Your increase in social status has declined your powers severely. And performing a ritual when you were already weakened took a bigger toll on you than before."

"Still think it's fun being an influencer?" Rhi asked with a teasing bump to the shoulder.

I was too exhausted to think up a comeback. It would have to wait.

"Come on, Rhi," Mom said. "Let's get her to her room. Sleep it off and we'll discuss training after." She directed the last part at me.

I nodded, in and out of consciousness as they moved me onto a blanket and enchanted the blanket to float up the stairs, like a magic carpet. Like floating on clouds, I'd traveled to a dreamlike state as I floated to my bed, the pillows enveloping me as they gently placed me down.

***

"No one has ever come back from the ghost realm," Mom had warned. Though, I didn't listen. In my mind, I would pull Wesley from his resentment, so Mom went along with it, helping me with "the plan."

After I'd woken up, I'd joined them downstairs to come up with a plan to help Wesley. He was dead, so there was no bringing him back, but we brainstormed potential ideas to bring *him* back, his personality. I couldn't bear to see that charming smile filled with resentment.

So, what was this plan?

I'd have to go back to being the outcast. The weird girl. Whatever. I'd done it all these years. What were a few more? Besides, I'd pretty much screwed myself on my friendship with Lindsay—who still wasn't answering my calls.

So, when I returned to school, I would work extra hard to be teased and taunted. This included humiliating myself any chance I could.

I walked into English that morning, taking the seat diagonal to Lindsay and slipping a note to her that had my sincerest apology for acting like a jerk. Even though I was supposed to go back to my outcast ways, I couldn't leave my tiff with Lindsay unresolved. She didn't deserve that.

She read the note and passed it to Rachel, who crumpled it up and threw it back to me. Again, I wrote another note apologizing.

Lindsay, I am genuinely sorry about what happened. You're a good friend, and I should have treated you better. If you really hate me that much, then I won't send you any more notes. I'll leave you alone. But I want you to know that I mean it. I really am sorry.

All I could do was hope for the best.

She took the note, this time not passing it to Rachel. She was writing back! I waited patiently, unfolding the note when she handed it to me.

Fine, but you're on probation. One more mess up and we aren't friends anymore. Agree?

Yes or No

She wanted me to circle one? Fine. I circled the yes and passed it back.

One problem resolved. Now, to start the humiliation…

God, why did I have to do this? The hardest part was letting go of my ego. Once I started, I'd be the laughingstock of the school. But I reminded myself, it was for Wesley. The guy who gave me a chance when no one else would. The person I'd let down. For him.

But before I did anything, I made a note on my phone to ask Mom if I could experiment with changing the source of our magic. I hated the thought of intentionally humiliating myself. There had to be another way. But for now…

Taking a deep breath, I raised my hand in the air.

"Yes, Isabel," the teacher said, pointing to me with her dry-erase marker.

Chewing on my bottom lip, I forced myself to do it. "Uhm. Can I go to the nurse? I have bad gas, and it's giving me a tummy ache."

The cackles already started. One guy even shouted out, "Oh, man" before he erupted into hysterical laughter, the class following his lead.

I'd purposely said *tummy*, much to Rhiannon's suggestion—to sound like a child—so I did. And jeez, was it humiliating.

The teacher's expression was unamused, shaking her head as she told me to go. I couldn't even look at her for the next part. Honestly, I'd debated not saying it at all, but Rhiannon insisted I did.

"Thank you, Mommy," I said before snatching the excuse note and darting out of the class, running straight to the bathroom to throw up—I'd been that nervous. Okay, maybe I didn't actually throw up, but man, did I feel stupid.

It worked, though. I could feel my magical energy surge within me, coursing through my body in small bursts.

Pushing through the bathroom door, I leaned against the wall, sinking to the floor. No way was I going to the nurse's office. I'd just sit here for the next hour until class let out.

Or that was the plan. In my haste, keeping my head down from sheer embarrassment, I'd managed to enter the *boy's* bathroom and only found out when I looked up to see a guy walking in.

"Uhh..." he said, cocking an eyebrow in confusion. "This isn't the girl's bathroom..." He eyed the urinals I'd completely missed when I powerwalked to the wall and put my head in my hands.

I forced a smile, shrugging as I stood. "My bad," I answered with nonchalance—though I was dying inside. If humiliation was what I was after, then I was off to a good start.

Leaving the bathroom, I wandered around the halls a bit to walk off my nerves. Catching my reflection in a window as I passed I noticed my face was burning bright from the humiliation. It was bad enough being the weird girl from the shunned family. Now I had to go out of my way to be mocked.

I walked to the stairs, ducking behind the stairwell to hide from the camera. Enchanting a piece of paper, I waved my hands to move the paper that floated through the air, covering the camera. That allowed me to step out from behind the stairwell to use magic from my seat on the step.

To practice my enchantment, I pulled out a pencil and eraser, placing them on the step beside me—while still holding the paper in place on the camera. I waved my hands over the pencil and eraser, watching them move and dance about. My fingers twirled in different directions, controlling them like puppets without strings.

Despite the rough start to my morning, playing with my magic made me feel lighter and free. Rhiannon was right. Accepting her magic made her feel peaceful, accepted in a different way. Happier.

When the bell rang, I collected my things and headed to my next class, where I practiced some more. I sat in the back with no one around me. So, I enchanted my eraser to dance around again, controlling my magic with ease. It came naturally to me the more I practiced, like any talent. Now that I'd mastered that useless talent, I was ready to take on the vampires.

If only it was so simple.

Every day for a week, I'd practiced in school, at home, anywhere I could slip it in. I didn't try summoning Wesley again. I wasn't ready for that. In addition to practicing, I kept up the embarrassment as often as possible, even resorting to picking my nose in front of a cute boy that played the tuba. I thought I'd keel over and die with that one, but Rhiannon helped me practice the night before. Yes, I'm aware of how ridiculous that was, but picking your nose in front of someone you think is cute is hard!

That Friday, I walked through the front door after school, inspired by a new plan.

"Mom? Rhi?" I called out, hoping they were both home. I had an idea to possibly get Wesley past his rage.

They both rushed into the room, thinking something was wrong. But I assured them, for once, things were going right.

"Can we do another ritual?" I asked, my tone eager. "I have an idea."

Rhiannon looked reluctant, but my mother's expression was pure joy and excitement. She loved seeing me interested in using my magic, so for me to tell her I *wanted* to perform a ritual was like I'd just agreed to join the family business.

"What's your idea?" she asked, motioning me to follow her into the kitchen to make some tea.

Before every ritual, she'd make us a calming tea to clear our minds and prepare us for using a vast amount of our magical energy. Though, with every ritual, I'd grown a bit stronger and figured out how to use this energy without it exhausting myself too much—aside from my encounter with Wesley on the phone. And now that I'd been growing my power all week, it would be even easier.

She boiled the water while Rhi and I sat at the kitchen table, our mugs and tea bags ready and our sugar and milk already in the cup.

"So, remember how you said that magic is manipulating energy?" I asked Rhi. She nodded, so I continued. "Well, I was thinking, what if we manipulated the energy within Wesley? If we could somehow change the negative energy consuming him, replace it with a more positive energy, maybe we can pull him out of the darkness."

I couldn't bring him back, but maybe I could bring him to the light.

"It's worth a try," Mom answered.

My eyes motioned to the tea. "Maybe you could use some of that calming magic you use for the tea on Wesley." I shrugged. "Maybe he won't be so bitter?"

We finished our tea and headed to the basement to prepare the ceremony. Mom and Rhiannon focused their magic on the communication aspect while I would focus my magical energy on replacing his anger with, well, *anything* else. Wesley appeared on the phone like before, screaming and cursing.

"Wesley," I said, my voice calm and filled with confidence. "Shut up for a second."

I could hear Rhiannon chuckle quietly beside me and forced myself to hold back the smile that crept on my lips.

Closing my eyes, I focused on the energy, absorbing the negativity and channeling it into the nearest object: that creepy wooden sign. I'd ask Mom what to do about that later.

Opening my eyes, I looked at Wesley, praying my theory was correct.

"Wesley?" I asked.

Chapter 9:

Matriarch

"Isabel?"

His voice was calm.

"Wesley?" I asked, treading carefully, testing the water. Just a dip of the toe before total submersion. "How are you feeling?"

Alas, his charming smile had returned. He rubbed his head, brushing past that flop of blond hair on his head. He laughed lightly and said, "I feel much better now."

Wesley! It was the old Wesley. Well, not the old. I mean, the guy was still a ghost, but he was no longer bitter and filled with rage. He was no longer calling me names and making cruel accusations.

My eyes teared up, beyond thrilled to have Wesley back. I touched the phone—the glass surface against the hard plastic. Nothing like the touch of his skin. No warmth or tingles. Only a cold glass surface.

Wesley's hand extended to the surface of the phone, touching mine. Curiously, I wondered why he had breached the surface before but not now.

Before the call disconnected, so to speak, I wanted to tell Wesley everything, explain to him what had happened.

"Wes, there are some things I need to tell you..."

***

"So you saw the vampires eating me?" he asked for the third time, astonished that I'd witnessed it before it happened.

"That's why I ran off so fast on our date. When I went to the bathroom and saw the vision, I freaked out. I'm sorry." Dipping my head in shame, I couldn't face him. Not after admitting I was the reason he was dead.

Wesley shook his head, touching the screen again. "No, I don't blame you. I'd have freaked out, too."

Again, my hand rested on the phone, on his—the only form of touch we could have. Though, it wasn't enough. I wanted to feel *him*, not the phone.

Those eyes returned to their previous blue mystique, pulling me into the oceanic abyss as they had in the car. Tilting my head slightly in awe, I watched him through the screen. His smile was filled with warmth and affection, eyes focused only on me. And for a moment, I'd forgotten anyone else was in the room as we exchanged smitten glances through the glass.

Rhiannon cleared her throat, bringing us back to reality. I'm sure Wesley had been just as lost in that moment as I had. "So, when did you actually die?" she asked.

"Yeah," I agreed, just as curious. "I'd been having those visions for a while, even while you were alive." I'd been totally oblivious that they were predicting his death. How stupid I'd been.

Wesley's eyebrows furrowed, realization hitting him. "I'm not sure," he answered, puzzled. "I don't remember. It's all so fuzzy. But it's coming back in pieces."

"That's expected," Mom answered. "You're only just now conscious after your death. You need time to remember, to piece it together. Like trying to remember a night after drinking."

Wesley's face lit up as it dawned on him. "Drinking!" he repeated. "I remember drinking with the guys that night of our date. And..." he paused, looking hard at nothing as he tried to remember. "I remember... sunrise... Amanda wouldn't stop clinging to me," he said with a shudder. "It was unbearable. The more she drank, the less she'd listen to my resistance. Even after I told her you were my date, and I wasn't interested in her."

"Aww," I cooed, touched by his confession. "You told her that? Even after I left?"

"Of course," Wesley answered, as if it were no brainer. "Just because you had to leave, doesn't make it okay to mess around with someone else."

Again, I was swept up in him, Rhiannon interjecting to bring us back. "Okay," she said, her tone a bit annoyed. "So when did you die?"

Wesley shrugged. "Not sure. But I'll tell you as soon as it comes to me."

Mom leaned forward to get his attention. "What should we tell your parents?" she asked, bringing up something that none of us had considered. "If we tell them you're dead, they'll want to know how we know and might not be too receptive to the truth. That we talked to your ghost through a smartphone. But if you could remember where your body is…" she suggested.

Wesley's face went blank as he realized the truth. "My parents think I'm missing," he pieced together. Maybe he hadn't realized he was dead. Or that the world had continued on without him. Or that his parents were still looking for him.

I could feel his despair, the way his shoulders slumped as reality settled in. Before, he was just an angry spirit, programmed to yell obscenities and nasty comments to those who spoke to him. But now that he was *reset*, and had started remembering bits of his life, he had realized what was going on.

"Don't tell them anything," he answered grimly. "I can't remember when or where I was killed. Saying something would only make you look suspicious. They'll arrest you, and then I won't be able to tell you who my killer was when I do remember. So just pretend you have no idea what happened to me for now."

I glanced at Mom and Rhi, who nodded in sync.

Changing the subject, he asked, "Do you know who the vampires are?"

I shook my head. "I only knew the one—Jack—when he attacked me. Honestly, I had no idea vampires even existed before that. I only just found out that I'm a witch."

"What about your visions?" he asked. "Do they reveal anything?"

"Not really. I can see the vampires but can't make out their faces. Their heads are always buried as they drank blood from—"

I looked away, unable to finish that sentence now that we knew who they were. Clearing my throat, I asked, "Do you remember who any of them are?"

"No. But if I remember anything, I'll let you know." His smile was weak, forced. "You know, if we get to talk again."

That seemed to be his only answer. But what else could he say? It wasn't like he could just walk down the street looking for clues. He was trapped in another realm. And his statement held truth. Would we talk again? This was new territory to me.

A headache formed and I swayed a bit from side to side. "I don't feel too well," I mumbled, my hand reaching my head and rubbing gently at my temples. I grew more lightheaded by the second.

"You've used a lot of power," Mom answered, her face tight with concern. "It's probably time to hang up and rest."

I nodded, remembering what happened last time. "I'll call you again soon, Wesley." I didn't want to hang up—not after I'd just got him back—but I had to.

Wesley smiled, assuring me he'd be waiting for my call, and I hung up.

Mom and Rhi helped me up the stairs again, walking with me to the couch. I plopped down, closing my eyes as Mom made me some more tea. Our signature drink. She'd enchanted it with something. Caffeine, maybe? Whatever she did to that tea, I felt loads better and sat up without issue.

Rhiannon sat on the chair across from me, silently stewing on something. I could tell she was bothered, though I wasn't entirely sure why. We'd made progress, right? Wasn't that worth celebrating?

I grabbed the pillow on the couch and chucked it at her. The pillow smacked the side of her head, falling to the floor. Rhiannon frowned, throwing it back. "What the hell?"

"That's what I'm saying," I countered. "What's up with you? Why are you sulking over there?"

"I'm not sulking," Rhi answered defensively.

My eyes narrowed, skeptical of her denial. And Mom? She was totally oblivious.

"I can't believe you combined spells and technology like that," she praised, taking a seat on the couch beside me. "That's the first time I've witnessed someone manipulate multiple spells with modifications. And you were such a natural. So innovative. Wasn't she, Rhi?"

Rhi nodded. "She was."

"Only training for a few weeks and already so gifted. Isn't that something?" She beamed with pride.

"Maybe Tink should take over as the next leader of the coven, then," Rhi suggested, peeking her eyes over her cup of tea as she took a sip.

"Oh, don't be silly, Rhi," Mom laughed. "You know you're next in line as coven matriarch."

Rhiannon sighed, placing her cup of tea on the table. "Yeah, but don't you think Tink would be a better option?"

"You know that's not how the coven works. You're next in line to—"

"To be the coven matriarch," Rhi repeated, cutting our mother off. "I know. But what if I don't want the position?"

Mom laughed, believing Rhi to be joking. But I could see it in her eyes—she was serious. "Why wouldn't you want to be coven leader?" Mom asked.

"I just want to be normal. I don't want magic. Or a coven. Or fighting vampires." Rhi looked away briefly, turning back to face us with glossy eyes. "I *hate* manipulating things—*people.*"

My mother's eyes met mine, shock filling us both. After she'd spent so long chastising my desire to leave my magic and be normal, she was now declaring it was *her* wish? I couldn't believe my ears!

"Rhi, where is this all coming from?" Mom asked. "You never felt this way before. Are you feeling neglected now that Isabel is experiencing her magic? It's alright to feel slighted—"

"No," she interrupted. "It isn't that. I've always hated magic. I *despise* it. I don't want it."

Mom's incredulous expression spoke volumes. That she just didn't understand. "Hate it? How could you hate it?"

On the verge of a breakdown, Mom was making it worse. I could tell Rhi was seconds from snapping, though I was just as confused as Mom. Why now? Why, all of a sudden, did she not want magic? Or should I say, why was she just now revealing it?

She looked away, but Mother pressed her harder, asking why again.

"Because I'm afraid!" she shrieked, jumping up from her chair. "I don't want to end up like Kevin! You think I want to go back to that? To exploiting people and using them?" Her voice cracked at the end, choked up on her emotions.

My mouth gaped open, unsure how to handle the situation. It'd been years since I'd seen Rhiannon freak out like this. In fact, thinking about it now, the last time she screamed like this was when she was dealing with all that crap she'd told me about in the car—when she discovered her magic and manipulated her friends.

The coffee table trembled, much as it had the night I ran home after Jack had tried to bite me. The lights flickered, the dingy chandelier swinging over the kitchen table in the other room.

Looking around the room, Rhi centered herself using her deep breathing techniques. The table stilled and the chandelier slowed to a stop.

In a calmer voice, she begged, "Please, Mom. Please, don't make me take over leadership of the coven. I don't want it. Like you said, she's gifted. Let her take the lead. She obviously would do better with it than I could. And despite what she says, I know she'd want it. She's a natural with magic."

Her words left me speechless. I had never once considered leading the coven. We'd never discussed the coven before. Heck, even the *word* coven was foreign in use until then. Honestly, the thought had never even crossed my mind—about the coven, let alone being a leader.

I was stunned by Rhi's confession, her fear. She was always so confident, so sure. Admitting to us now that it was never true, left me baffled.

Mom remained deep in thought, not speaking a word. But I knew Rhi desperately needed support in that moment, so I took the decision into my own hands.

"Of course, Rhi. Don't even worry about it. That or the rituals. Whatever you need, I got you."

Mom opened her mouth to speak, but I shot her a look that shut her up immediately, adding, "I didn't realize that magic made you feel that way. I'm sorry if I was pushing you too hard. Why didn't you say anything sooner?"

She sighed, rubbing her face with her hands. When she looked back up at me, her eyes were glossy with tears. "I didn't want to disappoint you guys. I was trying to be responsible, to sacrifice my own desires for what was right."

I shook my head, tsking at her. "But if it doesn't feel right for you, then it isn't right."

Mom excused herself politely, heading to the kitchen. No doubt, after that confession, she needed her own calming medication.

I took the opportunity to scoot to the edge of the couch, closer to Rhi. Grabbing her hands, my eyebrows rose, silently asking if she was alright.

Rhi looked at me with an expression of regret. "Do you think she's pissed?"

I waved my hand through the air, scoffing. "Ah, she'll get over it."

"And what about you?" Rhi asked, eyebrows creased in concern. In apprehension.

"Me?" I forced a laugh, hoping to lighten the mood. "I just got Wesley back to his old self. I'm feeling pretty freaking good. So, I think it's safe to say that I'll be alright, too." I gave her a wink to solidify my statement. "Seriously, don't worry about it. Me and Mom—we got this. Just take a step back from magic and focus on your art for a while."

She nodded, resolving she'd go up to her studio to work on this clay statue she'd been creating. As long as I could remember, Rhi had loved art and would use it to express herself.

In her absence, I leaned back against the couch, repeating the phrase in my mind. *Coven matriarch.* Just what did that entail?

Chapter 10:

Growth

Knowing Rhi didn't want to do magic anymore meant that I needed to step up to take her place. Without her help in the rituals, I needed to be stronger, which meant distancing myself from my friends. Lindsay in particular. Rachel and Amanda—I knew they could take me or leave me. Honestly, they'd probably prefer I disappeared. But Lindsay had fallen right back into our usual routine of friendship.

I refused to just end what we had without explanation. However, I couldn't exactly say, *Hey, we can't hang out for a while because I need to grow my magical powers.* The only way I could gain some distance without completely ruining my friendship with Lindsay—which was something she didn't deserve—was to take baby steps.

As much as I didn't want to, I told them I was busy after school helping Mom with her online business. In a sense, it was true. I mean, I did help her enchant the garden and products we sold.

Easing myself away, I spent less and less time with them, until we only spoke now and again in English and in the hallway. If I pulled away all at once, Lindsay would assume she'd done something wrong, and I didn't want to hurt her.

After school, I trained with Mom and Rhiannon more than ever before. Though Rhi hadn't been doing magic like she had before, she was there for guidance, to help me and offer advice and feedback when I practiced magic.

And in her spare time, Rhi kept working on her art—her clay statue. She'd only recently started using clay a month or so ago. She'd created a few flower pots and trinket dishes, expanding to more and more items.

Once Mom accepted Rhi's confession, she suggested that Rhi's art be added to their inventory to sell. Rhi was thrilled with the idea, staying involved but not having to do magic. And in the past week, I saw a whole new Rhi, exuding a happiness I didn't know she had been lacking.

My visions had completely ceased. Not a single one had appeared since I spoke with Wesley, which was a major relief. But it also left me uneasy. Now that I realized those visions were real, a prophecy, I *wanted* to receive them, hoping I could find out some information about the vampires. Now that I knew what I was looking for, they stopped.

Why?

I had even tried meditation with Rhi, hoping it would open my mind or some nonsense. But still, nothing.

Despite my daily training, my constant humiliation and teasing at school, Mom said I wasn't strong enough to take on the vampires anyway. How much more did I need? I'd grown much stronger—stronger than I'd ever been—and it wasn't enough? Didn't she tell me I was a natural?

"Mom, isn't there another source of power for our magic?" I asked. Already knowing her answer, I quickly added, "I mean, haven't you ever experimented? *Tried* to find something else?"

Mom shook her head. "Absolutely not. This is our source of power. It has been for generations. You may have made some changes to spells, but don't get a big head about this, Isabel. Our source of magic is what it is, and it cannot be changed."

"But why not?" I protested, not believing this was the only way. "You said it yourself, I'm strong. Maybe I could find another way to gain power."

"You think you're strong?" she asked, huffing a laugh. "This is *nothing* compared to the power you could have."

Cocky, overexerting my confidence, I answered, "You said that you'd never seen someone pulled out of their rage like that." As if that answer would be the mic drop I'd expected.

But again, Mom laughed but was less sarcastic and more of a genuine, hearty chuckle—which was worse. "Okay. But can you do this?"

Her hands rose in the air, fingers pulling invisible strings of control. The plants that were hung along the kitchen windowsills sprang to life, rapidly growing through the house in a matter of seconds. Peering outside the window, the garden bloomed with flowers, ripe tomatoes, strawberries—all of it! Everything was suddenly plump and full, as if spring had just hit and everything was in bloom.

Was that how she managed to keep the garden growing year-round for business?

Rhiannon burst through the door, pointing outside. "Oh my God, did you guys see that? Everything outside just bloomed in a matter of seconds!"

Mom side-eyed me, snickering when Rhi's eyes widened at the image inside the house. At the plants that had crept along the walls and floor, taking over the house like it had been abandoned and left in the wild for decades.

"You like that trick? How about this?" Mom raised her hands again and our run-down home slowly morphed into a brand new one, the changes taking place in front of our very eyes.

Stains on the carpet disappeared along with the spots on the wall. The cobwebs and dust that had settled years before were whisked away, dissolving into nothing. Broken boards fused together in repair.

Everything was *clean*. New.

Unfolding before my eyes, I watched as the walls shined brighter with a fresh color of paint—but without the smell. Even the tears in the furniture had been stitched together, ceasing to exist.

It was like watching the sped-up version of the HGTV channel.

Mom stumbled to the side, losing her footing but catching herself on the back of the chair. The new chair that hardly resembled the old one.

Sitting down, she rubbed her head, her voice strained as she asked, "Can you do that, Isabel?"

Point proven.

But I couldn't respond. I was still speechlessly gawking at the house. However, she answered for me.

"You can't. Which is why you need more power." She shifted, groaning as she did. "You've unlocked only a fraction of the power within. But you'll never be this strong if you keep maintaining your friendships. Going out, gossiping with those girls… you're making yourself weak. I know it's what you want, but magic requires sacrifice."

I shook my head—partially to shake myself free of my shock—and stepped closer. "I've pretty much stopped talking to them. We barely say hi now."

Mom nodded, her eyebrows pulled in tight, as if in pain. Her voice was weak when she said, "This," motioning around her, "is only a drop in the ocean. At peak strength, you could be unstoppable. But you still have a ways to go." She pointed to a plant nearby. "Go on. Try to make it grow."

I focused on the plant, holding out my palms to make it grow. Squinting in concentration, I tried and tried, but nothing happened.

After a moment, Mom stood from her chair, but her balance was still off, and she began to fall. In the midst of fainting, Rhiannon dashed toward her, catching her. I jumped up, helping Rhiannon carry her to the couch.

She lay there for a minute with her eyes closed.

"I've never seen her use this much power," Rhi whispered, looking to me with concern in her eyes. "I didn't even know she could."

Mom's eyes peeked open, and she grabbed my locket, holding it in her palm. "Use this locket to channel your power, and you'll be even stronger. Once you remove all your friendships, you'll have more power than you could imagine."

I looked away, dreading the words. Sure, Lindsay and I hadn't been talking as much as before but shutting her out completely made my heart sink. To give up the one true friendship I'd had outside of my own family filled me with dread.

"I know it's hard," Mom said, "but it's important. To be strong enough to fight and lead, you need to do this."

"Magic requires sacrifice," I mumbled in acknowledgment.

The following day at school, Rhiannon accompanied me in the morning. The plan was for her to come in to "reminisce" about her time there. Though, it was the rumor she planned to start that was the true intention of her being there.

We walked the halls together, and for a moment, it reminded me of the days when we would go to school together, hanging out in the morning and between classes, eating lunch together. I missed those days, before I was alone.

As planned, I excused myself to go to the bathroom, and she used the opportunity to create some elaborate, embarrassing, rumor. I hoped that she would go with the time shaved off my eyebrows, and not the time I crapped my pants on the field trip to the pumpkin patch.

Really, it didn't matter. The stronger the humiliation, the more my power grew. And at this point, I'd become somewhat immune to the teasing. In fact, I found it comical and got a kick out of creating awkward situations to incite teasing. It took a lot of practice, but Rhi showed me how to have fun with it, to be the one to instigate it. Because at least if I'm the one instigating it, I could have some control over what they teased me about.

I was still in the bathroom when I felt my power growing, knowing the rumor had been planted, the seed spreading from person to person in a matter of minutes.

When I stepped out of the bathroom, Rhi winked, whispering that it was done. She bid me goodbye and walked away. As she did, some guy whistled, making some lewd comment, but she waved him off and continued walking.

Dang, I wanted that kind of confidence.

When I got home, the first thing I did was communicate with Wesley. This time, I did it without the help of Mom or Rhiannon, and without the chanting we'd done each time before.

It was a whim, but it worked.

"Isabel," he answered, appearing on the screen. His voice was soft, excited to see me. "I've missed you."

"I've missed you, too," I said with a giggle, thinking of how much we sounded like a typical teenage couple. Only, we weren't dating and he was, you know, a dead ghost in a phone. But circumstances aside, it felt normal.

"I have news," he said, his face growing serious, though still enthusiastic. "I've learned a new trick to this realm. I can eavesdrop on other devices now that I'm not shrouded with rage."

My jaw dropped. "Seriously?" I had no idea that was even possible.

"It's crazy, isn't it? But now I can keep an eye on the other side for you. Maybe I can help you figure out who the vampires are. Speaking of which, have you discovered any new information? I think I've remembered a few details that might help."

His mouth ran a mile a minute, quickly bringing me up to speed—if only I could keep up.

I chuckled, shaking my head. "Wesley, slow down. One thing at a time. What did you remember?"

His cheeks blushed—which I didn't know was possible without the blood flow of a living person. Maybe it was the embodiment of him of his emotions that made such things work.

"Sorry. I guess I was so excited to see you, I couldn't slow myself down."

God, how could someone hurt this guy? He was sweeter than cookie dough. It broke my heart to think anyone could have ill intentions for him.

"I remember leaving the morning after the party, looking for my phone. A few of the guys went with me to the park, hoping it might be there. I think… maybe… we went to the park before the party?" Wesley was guessing at that last part, but going to the park the morning after, he'd remembered that with certainty. "So, maybe check out the park."

I nodded, thinking it over. "Makes sense. That was where Jack took me."

Wesley's face morphed into a frown at the mention of Jack—his presumed friend before all this vampire mess. Had he felt more betrayed that his friend was working with the enemy, or that he tried to kill me? Either way, Wesley was never too pleased when Jack's name was mentioned.

I'd debated mentioning more about the dance, our date, wanting to tell Wesley how kind he'd been to me and how much it was appreciated, but every phone call held limited time to speak as it exhausted me, so I needed to move onto the more pressing matters.

"I've been thinking; if we can manipulate the energy to use a phone, could it be done with a TV? I mean, if I could see visions through the mirror, why not a big ol' flat screen to make it easier?"

Wesley shrugged, unsure of the answer but pleased that I'd asked him. Maybe he just wanted to be involved with something since the other realm was probably filled with dreadful ghosts—not that I'd asked him about it. You know, limited time speaking and all.

"Have you seen anything when you were spying on other devices?" I asked.

"Nothing concrete, but you might want to take a closer look at the team. I've overheard them talk about missing kids, in a joking manner. Something tells me they're involved."

I nodded, making a note of it on the sticky pad near my bed. "They *were* the ones insisting you ran away. Said you talked about it often, going back to the city."

Wesley looked away, his hand rubbing the back of his neck. "I did when I first moved here. But I hadn't mentioned it since those first few weeks. Honestly, I liked this town. Sure, it was smaller than what I was used to, but it has its own charm. I guess I could see why they'd think that, but I still think there's something fishy going on with the team."

"Then that's who I'll check out first," I resolved, knowing what was next to come. It didn't sit well with me, but I needed to do it. "Wesley, I need to hang up the call now."

Disappointment covered his face, knowing he'd be sent back to his realm, but he forced a smile and nodded. "I understand. Don't want you to use up all your power talking to me. Go try your TV idea and see if you can watch someone from the team. Maybe start with Danny since he's the quarterback. He'd probably know the most."

I nodded, holding back how discouraged and reluctant I was to hang up, replacing it with a sad smile. "I'll call you soon and tell you what I find out."

His charming smile had returned—the one that made me swoon over him—and he said, "I'll be waiting." The way he said it made my heart beat faster, like when we'd been in the car together.

"I'll talk to you then," I said, ending the call.

I rushed downstairs to tell Mom and Rhiannon my idea about the TV. Since I no longer had visions coming through, maybe I could peek at these vampires through the screen instead.

Mom nodded slowly. "You won't be able to watch the vampire," she said after a moment, deflating my ego for the second time that week.

"Why not?"

"To peek in on someone's life like that, you need to know their name, their face. You must know their identity to reach out and watch. Without that information, we can't see the vampire."

Dang. Always something.

"Well, I can watch Danny, right? Wesley said to check with the team, that they might know more than they let on. So, theoretically speaking, I could watch Danny on the TV?" I asked, piecing it together.

Mom nodded. "You could. Just know that when you watch someone, you're invading their privacy. You might see something you don't want to see. Hear conversations not meant for your ears."

Rhiannon added, "Would you want someone watching you without your knowledge? It all seems so sketchy to me."

I shook my head, determined to do something, even if they weren't fully on board. "I'll do whatever it takes to find out who killed Wesley. Besides, how does the saying go? *Don't do anything you wouldn't want on the front page of the newspaper* or something?"

Rhiannon sighed, uneasy with the idea but curious to know more. She hated the manipulation of magic and how it affected people. But I knew she wanted to help Wesley, to stop the vampires from killing anyone else. And knowing that there were more students missing, and possibly more to come, she resolved that she'd help.

The three of us gathered around the living room, situating ourselves in front of the TV.

"I guess we won't be needing these," Rhi teased, pointing to the stack of DVDs.

When Mom had used her magic to change the house around, she'd also turned the TV into a big flat-screen smart TV. No longer would we need to watch the much smaller box TV from the 90s.

Mom lit her candles and began her chanting, but I stopped her mid-chant. "Actually, I was able to connect with Wesley without the candles and chanting," I said.

She shook her head. "The candles are for protection. The chanting is to communicate with our ancestors and ask for their assistance. I don't do it because I *need* to, I do it for an added layer of help in case something happens when using my magic has made me weaker."

"Ah," I said with a nod, taking my seat on the floor. We could've sat on the couch, but I had too much nervous energy to sit there. I needed to be closer, to watch from only a few feet away like when I'd sit with my legs crossed as a child watching cartoons.

"What was his name again?" Mom asked. "The boy you wanted to watch?"

"Danny. Danny Miller."

"We call upon Danny Miller," she sang out, her voice lower, deeper, as if we were calling out to the dead during a séance.

The TV flickered to life, static covering the previously dark screen. Rhi and I jumped, looking at one another in astonishment. She wasn't using her magic but was holding my hand so I could absorb it and use it if I got too weak.

Images appeared on the screen, the white and black static slowly morphing into a person. Voices rang out, muffled at first, but even that became clear after a moment. Slowly, the screen merged into what looked like a television show—only it wasn't.

It was Danny. Sitting in his car with Rachel. Kissing.

Ew!

I scoffed, grossed out by the image and forced myself not to look away. *Please don't let them move to the back seat.*

Glancing at my mother, she wore an *I told you* expression. Yeah, yeah, I saw something that wasn't meant for my eyes. Please let it be over soon. Grabbing the remote, I paused the screen, waiting a few minutes for their moment to pass so I could fast forward past the kissing, earning a scolding glare from Rhi.

After a moment, Rachel leaned back in the seat, pulling down the visor to adjust her lipstick. At least that meant they were probably done kissing.

They spent the next few minutes talking about boring school things. The winter formal coming up in the next month, the football team practicing for the championship game, which would be happening in only a few weeks, and a bunch of other things that made me yawn.

"We're getting nowhere," I whined. Mom shushed me as she listened intently. Glad she could find it so interesting because I was bored out of my skull with their talk of everyday stuff.

The screen started to go fuzzy around the edges and my mother warned, "Our powers are depleting."

Our powers are depleting? There must be a better way to get power. This felt so manual and inefficient. Still, I nodded, thinking this had been a waste of time anyway. But as static slowly expanded on the screen, the conversation turned.

"Can you believe Coach wants to find someone else to replace Wesley for the championship game?" Danny said to Rachel.

My ears perked up and I leaned forward, brought to life at the mention of Wesley's name.

"In the middle of the season?" she asked.

"I know! It's crazy, right? He wants us to give them a good ol' initiation at the park, like we do with everyone new to the team."

The park. He said the park. The same place where Wesley said to look, where Jack had attacked me.

"Well, I know you got it, babe. You're the quarterback for a reason."

I rolled my eyes as Danny flexed his chest and muscles, his ego inflated by Rachel's comment.

"So, when are you going?" she asked.

Finally, we were getting somewhere. But the dang TV had been overrun with static until I couldn't hear anything besides the white noise from the static. The image had shrunk to nothing but static, ending our "show," if you could call it that.

When it ended, I insisted we go to the park and wait to see if anyone would come. Mom claimed it was too dangerous, and that we needed to just sit back and wait for our powers to replenish. If we stumbled upon a coven of vampires, what would we do without our strength? It would be too dangerous.

But sitting here waiting was too dangerous. By doing nothing, we were risking more people being taken and harmed. Killed. Turned into vampires. Whatever they were doing, sitting around meant it would happen again and again until we put a stop to it.

That was why I snuck to Rhiannon's room that night, begging her to sneak out with me to the park.

"Please," I begged. "Just a quick look around and we'll leave. I just want to see if there are any clues about Wesley's death."

"In the dark?"

"I can't wait until morning. I won't be able to sleep until I at least look." Biscuits, who had jumped from her bed to my lap, started to growl lowly in his throat. His tail swished agitatedly as he looked at me.

Reluctantly—and after 15 minutes of my begging and ignoring Biscuits—she agreed, driving us out "for milkshakes," as she told Mom, who insisted we bring her back a vanilla.

At the park, we crept along the trail, using our phones to light the path.

"This was where Jack brought me," I said, gesturing to the bench we'd sat on. I crouched down, looking at the ground, inspecting for blood or something—anything to reveal Wesley had died there. But I was coming up empty. Maybe Wesley had died in the locker room, where the visions took place. Then, what was his feeling about the park?

136

"I'm not seeing anything," Rhiannon said after 10 minutes of looking. "We need to get back soon or Mom will be suspicious. We still need to bring her back a vanilla, remember?"

I nodded, knowing she was right. "Fine, but I'm coming back in the daylight."

We walked back toward the car but heard a rustle in the leaves. Both of us froze in place, not moving or speaking. We covered our lights with our fingers, not giving ourselves away in case it was vampires.

Again, we heard a rustle, accompanied by the snapping of twigs on the ground.

"Someone's here," I whispered, looking around but seeing nothing in the dark. Not even the moon was enough to illuminate the path. "What do we d—"

Something plowed into my side, knocking me to the ground.

"Tink!" Rhiannon screamed, shining her light on me and… a vampire?

I knew it! I freaking knew there was something going on here!

Fangs glinted in the light, though his face was unrecognizable. A vampire I didn't know.

"Finally, a Dufort within my grasp," he said, hissing like an animal. "Think you can stop us? We're everywhere!"

Another vampire emerged from the tree line, and who knew if there were more.

His mouth edged closer to my throat, fangs dripping with saliva. My heart pounded furiously, which he only enjoyed more, running his finger along my chest to the exact spot where my heart lay beneath my skin.

"Get away from me!" Rhi shouted in the background, fighting off the other vampire. But her powers had weakened from disuse.

Using my magic, I enchanted a tree branch to break off and clock him in the head, knocking him away from my sister. Lifting the same tree branch, I enchanted it to strike the vampire that had me pinned to the ground.

It knocked him off, giving me the opportunity to jump up and clutch my phone with one hand as I grabbed the vampire with the other. The power channeled through my body, through my limbs, to the fingertips that were closed around his arm.

"Burn!" I shouted, enchanting the technology to shine light on the vampire. The phone glowed, sending the power through me, searing the vampire's skin. He squealed and howled in the most animalistic way, his skin burning to a crisp, turning to dust.

The other vampire lunged at me, realizing that *I* was the threat, not Rhiannon. He tackled me, his fangs diving for my chest, wasting no time like the other vampire had.

Rhiannon grabbed a branch and used it to wail on him, knocking him off me. Unable to get to my feet, I climbed over him to hold him in place, pressing my locket to his forehead.

"Burn, dammit!"

He, too, squealed and screeched, writhing in pain as he dissolved into nothing.

"Do you think there are more?" I asked as Rhi grabbed my hand and pulled me to my feet.

"Who knows. Let's get the hell out of here."

She didn't wait for my response before dragging me along the path, not letting go of my hand. I was with her on escaping. No way did I want to be outnumbered by vampires.

But as we ran to the car, I noticed someone in the woods. Someone familiar.

"Wait!" I shouted. Jerking her back, I stopped running, squinting my eyes as I looked through the darkness. Shining my light around, I didn't see anything.

"What was it?" she asked, but all I could do was stare.

I *knew* I saw something. I knew it but nothing was there now.

"I thought I saw a boy from school. Uh... um..." What was his name? Somehow, I always forgot it. Really, I'd always forgotten his existence until I saw him again. Snapping my fingers, I said, "James. I saw James."

"Who's James?"

"Don't you listen? A boy from school?"

Rhiannon looked around the darkness, at the trees and bushes, the branches and twigs. No one. Nothing.

"Well, he's gone now so let's go."

I wasn't as quick to move, hoping that if he was there, he would be alright. But as I ran off, I couldn't remember what I'd just been thinking about.

Had I seen someone? Maybe my mind was playing tricks on me. There was no way... what was his name? Was it even a he? Everything seemed so confusing now. What was I doing after the vampires attacked? I'd stopped... but why? I couldn't remember.

We headed to the diner to get the milkshakes as promised. Plus, after all that, we deserved to have some kind of treat. Rhiannon insisted we tell Mom about what happened, but I didn't think that was smart. She'd just freak out.

After we'd calmed down enough to head back without suspicion, we ordered Mom's vanilla and drove home.

But the ride home left me uneasy. *Why did I stop in the woods back there?* The question kept repeating in my mind, but it was like my memory had been left blank. Like it was a disc with a scratch and all you could do was play the next song, the next scene, skipping over the blip that didn't work.

What was I doing in the woods?

Chapter 11:

Attack

After that night in the park—when I took down not one but *two* vampires—my confidence skyrocketed, making me feel capable of taking on anything. And with this newfound confidence, I'd practiced religiously, growing stronger than even I thought possible. Since that night in the woods, I'd gotten a good grasp on my powers, growing stronger with the amplified teasing at school and the continual practice at home.

In fact, I felt so certain in my abilities that I started to actively seek out the vampires. With Wesley on the phone, I'd enchant the television to peek in on different suspects. Sometimes, Mom or Rhi sat with me, taking notes on anything that stood out. Other times, it was just me and Wesley.

What I knew so far, Danny was no vampire leader. Honestly, the guy was a bit dim. I didn't see him as someone who could orchestrate something as intricate as killing people without getting caught.

That isn't to say he wasn't involved in *some* way. Not that he was a vampire, but some of the things he'd said to Wesley didn't entirely match up to what we'd seen. For instance, Danny was a lot closer with the coach than he'd let on.

The night of the dance, Wesley had asked Danny why the coach insisted they all dress in the same costume. Danny talked trash about the coach, going on about how he was such a tool and how he couldn't stand him. Yet, when we peeked in on Danny's life, it turned out he was quite friendly with the coach.

Why lie about something like that? Just what else was he hiding?

I would have assumed he just didn't want to admit it because it made him look "uncool" or something, but it was the way he went about it. Before meeting with the coach in the locker room, he'd look down both ends of the hall, waiting before entering if anyone else was around. Why do that if you were just meeting with the coach?

But it was what would happen next that had me suspecting Danny and the coach. When he'd enter the locker room, he would approach the coach, and then the edges of the screen would darken, as if someone turned on the vignette filter. Someone else would appear, though they would always be at the corners of the screen where it was darkest, and I was unable to make out who the figure was.

I sat on the couch in the basement where our altar previously sat. Insisting we did a little rearranging, the altar was now at the other end of the basement to make room for the TV I begged Mom to buy. On the way back from buying a new flat screen—because no one sold box TVs anymore—we stopped by a thrift shop in the next town over, bringing home a leather loveseat.

Wesley was propped up on a pillow, the phone at an angle to face both me and the television. In a way, it felt like he was in the room with me, for real. Only, I couldn't feel his touch, the warmth from his presence. Silently, I had vowed that I would find a way to bring him back once we got this vampire nonsense squared away.

With a bowl of popcorn in my lap, I popped a piece into my mouth, Wesley groaning in jealousy.

"Quit fussing," I teased, tossing a piece at the phone. "You don't even like kettle corn."

He rolled his eyes, trying to reach through the phone for the piece. We'd yet to figure out why he could reach through before but not now. Mom said that restoring his consciousness must have made him incapable somehow.

Magic… Sometimes it didn't make sense. Or we just didn't understand it.

"It's an unwritten rule: you need to have butter on your popcorn," Wesley joked, his lips curved at the corner in a charming smirk. "But even I'd eat that junk right now. Honestly, I'd take that brown glop from the cafeteria if it meant I could eat again. I don't really feel hungry, but I miss the taste of food. Even meatloaf," he said, his nose scrunched up in disgust.

I laughed, though it felt hollow. Wesley couldn't even eat good food in the ghost realm. He couldn't feel the warmth of the sun or breeze, hug his parents, go bowling or play games at the arcade. He was stuck in a world he never asked to be in.

I'll get you out, Wesley. One way or another, I'll do it.

"Okay, shh," I said, holding a finger to my mouth. "We're getting to the good part."

You'd think we were watching a regular movie, but nope. We were spying on Clayton, a guy on the team who I overheard planning a meeting with the coach about his performance on the team. Maybe it really was just a meeting about football, but I was about to find out.

Clayton walked into the locker room, looking around in confusion at the darkness. "Hello?" he called out, switching on the light to reveal the coach and a few guys from the team.

I leaned forward, my eyebrows pulled in tight enough to give me a headache. Grabbing my pen and paper, I jotted down the date and time.

"Clayton. I'm glad you're here," Coach said, taking a step toward the kid. "The tasks we'd discussed previously have been plotted out and are ready to be executed. Do you remember your position?"

The coach spoke as if he were reading a script, his tone rigid and monotonous. It was as if someone were guiding him, telling him what to say. The coach I'd met had never been *Shakespearean*, to put it nicely.

Was he talking about football? Maybe. Their executed tasks could refer to their positions on the field. But something in my gut insisted it was something else, something darker.

Clayton nodded. "I remember. You want me on the beach of Lake Michigan and—"

"Shut your mouth!" the coach snapped. "You don't speak of it out loud. Always assume your enemies are watching and listening. You will go to your designated position at exactly 19:00 hours."

Clayton's head tilted, mouth gaped open in confusion.

Sighing, the coach pinched the bridge of his nose. "Seven o'clock," he answered, dumbing it down for the boy, adding in "p.m." for good measure.

The coach faced the ominous figure in the corner, shrouded in darkness. "Is that all?" he asked. But before I could hear an answer from the figure, the screen crackled and popped like a fire, the edges burning until only ash remained on the screen, going dark and silent.

I turned to face Wesley, his eyes widened in shock. "There's no way that meeting was about football," he said, his voice breathless as he stared at the blank television screen. Jerking his gaze to mine, he asked, "What do you think they're planning on the beach?"

I shrugged. "Only one way to find out."

"You're not going there, are you?"

Nodding, I said, "I have to. If they're planning something bad, something deadly, then I need to stop them."

"No, Isabel. That's insane. You could be killed. You have no idea what they're planning or how many of them are there. They could overpower you."

"I can't do nothing, Wes. What if they're planning to kill someone? Am I supposed to just sit back and watch them?" *Like I did with you?* I couldn't express the thought out loud, but it was there, present in the tense air. Even without him physically in the room with me, he knew what I hadn't been able to say.

"Isabel, listen to me. It wasn't your fault they killed me. But if you go running after them, they might kill you, too. Please, don't go."

I knew why Wesley felt that way, but he was wrong. It was my fault. Trying to make me feel better about the truth didn't change it. I *had* to do this. Even if it meant being in danger, I couldn't let them get away with hurting anyone else.

"I'm sorry, Wesley. I can't do nothing," I repeated, standing from the couch and grabbing the phone. "I'll call you back later, when I get back. Because I *am* coming back. Remember, two vampires," I teased to lighten the conversation.

"Isabel, don't be stupid! You lucked out before, but it might not happen again. If you're not going to listen to me, at least bring Rhi and your mom with you."

I forced a smile, saying, "I'll talk to you later, Peacock Boy," before I hung up the phone. Let him believe I took them with me. It might ease his mind a bit. Though, I had no intention of bringing anyone else along.

Rhiannon made it clear she wanted nothing to do with this anymore, and Mom would only stop me. This, I needed to figure out on my own.

I waited until an hour before seven and headed toward the beach, knowing it would take a while to get there—especially without a ride from Rhiannon.

With stealth, I slipped out the back door and to the shed, grabbing the bike that sat in the back corner collecting dust for the past few years. I walked the bike to the edge of the forest as I snuck away, only pedaling after I was enveloped by the trees.

Riding a bike over the bumpy ground and various twigs was difficult until I reached the trails.

I rode for nearly an hour, finally slowing down as I neared the beach. Whipping my phone from my pocket, I used my powers to connect to Clayton, watching him like I did on television, though on a much smaller screen.

Clayton appeared on the screen, hunkered down behind the tall grass, watching a woman jogging along the beach in the sand. Darkness had claimed the sky, so he was unseen to the woman, despite his head poking out above the tall blades.

I tried to get an idea of his position—a noteworthy tree or sand dune—but everything looked the same from where I stood to where he did. How far along the beach was he?

As the woman neared him, he sprung from the bushes, lunging toward her and knocking her to the ground. The woman was frozen in fear, too terrified to fight him off.

Ending my powers on the phone, I sprinted down the beach, hoping I'd chosen the right direction to go.

The screams led me to them, and it didn't take long before I found him on top of the woman, her arms pinned above her head as he inhaled her scent, licking his lips. A shudder of disgust rolled through me. I ran up and tackled him to the ground, releasing the woman who blinked and stared, not moving.

"You little bitch!" Clayton growled, jumping to his feet and charging for me. He knocked me to the ground, fangs glistening in the moonlight, slowly inching toward my neck.

No!

I grunted, attempting to push him away, but he was too strong. His hands gripped my wrists, holding me in place just as he had the woman. Without my magic, I'd be helpless. But I wasn't helpless. I enchanted his shirt to yank over his head, covering his eyes.

The action took him by surprise, and he quickly released my wrists to pull his shirt away, giving me an opening to push him off me, skittering to my feet. He lunged for me, and I barely dodged his attack, his fingernails slicing into my arm as he tried to grab me.

I waved my hands through the air, enchanting the sand into a small sandstorm, covering only the few feet surrounding us. Grabbing my locket, I held it out, begging the light to grow as it had before.

"Burn him!" I demanded but the locket remained silent to my request.

He jumped forward, emerging from the sandstorm. Grabbing my shoulder, he held me in place, shoving my head to the side as he attempted to bury his teeth in my neck. With the locket in my hand, I pressed it against his cheek, searing the skin in a repulsive sizzle that stank of burned skin. Stumbling backward, he fell to the ground, gripping his cheek.

I held out the locket, demanding once more—but with more determination—to "Burn him!" The locket glowed dimly at first. But the more I imagined him burning, his body erupting in flames, the brighter it glowed until his skin turned crisp and burned, disintegrating to dust.

Shaking my head, I turned to the woman that cowered in the sand, crouching down beside her. "Are you alright?" I asked in a soothing tone, but she'd become hysterical. This woman who wouldn't even fight had begun to thrash her limbs in every direction, screeching for me to get away.

How ungrateful! I'd just saved her, and she thought I was with *them*? "Please," I begged, urging her to calm down, but she scrambled to her feet, ready to run.

Popping out from behind the tall weeds, Rhi grabbed the woman, telling her to forget everything that had happened. I could sense the magic that seeped from Rhi's grasp, enchanting the woman's memory—something I didn't know was possible.

She stopped screaming, her eyes emotionless as she nodded blankly.

"On your way, then," Rhi said, motioning to the beach.

The woman continued jogging along, as if she hadn't just been attacked by a vampire and watched him disintegrate in front of her.

"How the… What the… *How?*" I asked, my jaw so wide, it hit the sand and took in the tides.

Rhi answered, "Mom taught me. Now, grab your bike, and let's head back to the car before more vamps show up."

I nodded, heading down the beach as I scoured the various weeds, looking for where I'd left my bike. But I was still in shock that Rhi had appeared. "How did you know I was out here?"

She snorted in amusement. "Please, girl. You are anything but discreet. I heard you talking with Wesley, so I followed you out here. You're not the only one who can sneak around."

She gave me a wink to lighten the mood, though I could sense that she was pretty annoyed with my actions.

"I thought you hated using magic," I said, replaying the way she'd made that woman forget what she saw.

"I do. But I wasn't about to let her run off and scare the whole town with tales of vampires. Like they would've believed her. If anything, they'd call her crazy and mock her like they do us. Figured it might be better for her to just forget, rather than be shunned."

Rhi sighed, looking out at the lake, the moonlight reflecting across the water. "To be honest, it's not the magic I hate, it's the manipulation. Who am I to take away her memories?"

"You did so for her own good, to keep her safe and happy," I reasoned, defending her actions.

"That was the intention. But who am I to make that decision? How do I know that was what's best for her? Sometimes, what seems like the best option really isn't. We assume it's because it makes us happier, but maybe we need that disappointment to grow."

I watched her staring out at the water in silence and I realized...

"We're not talking about the woman anymore, are we?"

With a subtle shake of her head, she said, "Nope."

I grabbed her hand, plopping into the sand and pulling her down with me.

"What the—" she called out as she fell on her butt into the sand.

"Ouch. Could've been a little easier with that landing," I teased, bumping her shoulder when she straightened herself.

She grumbled, "You didn't give me much choice."

I shrugged, leaning back to rest on my arms as I watched the waves pull in and out, nearly touching our feet. "I thought maybe we should have a chat. A little sisterly bonding."

I waited for her to explain her statement, but she didn't. So, I urged her along. "What's on your mind?"

She blew out a breath, her face pained in conflict. "You remember my boyfriend a few years ago?"

I nodded. "Yeah. You guys were super close."

"That's what I thought, too. But the truth was, he was a master of manipulation. He was the reason I became that person I hated so much. The one who was conniving and manipulative like him. He's the one who distanced me from my friends and told me to lie. He'd made me believe that if I really loved him, then I would do these things for him. He knew just what to say to make me feel bad about telling him no. He eventually took me to a place where I couldn't make a decision without him."

I blew out an irritated breath. "What a jerk."

"He was. But I should have known better. I should have told him off when he asked me to lie and manipulate. When he threatened and blackmailed me, I should have just kicked him in the groin."

She laughed at that part, but there was no real humor in it. Her lip still trembled with emotion, her voice uneven as she spoke. She was still just as affected by this as she had been back then.

"You can't blame yourself. You didn't know what he was doing."

"Not at first. It started small, subtle. If I wanted to hang out with my friends when he wanted to hang out with me, he'd guilt me. 'Don't you want to spend time with me?' he'd ask. 'You see your friends all the time, and I just want to be with you.'"

She scoffed.

I wrapped my arm around her shoulder, pulling her in for a hug. What was intended as only a few minutes of sitting in the sand had turned into an hour. Rhiannon and I had the first *real* talk we'd had in a while. One in which we were open and vulnerable, with no apologies for our thoughts. We were just... honest. About our past and our present. And even our future.

"What I really want is to help people," she said when we got on the topic of college. "Maybe a degree in humanities with a minor in art. Or vice versa," she said, her eyes glazing over as she visualized it.

"This is when Mom would say *helping people is in our blood*," I said with a chuckle.

Rhi straightened up, leaning forward with an excited grin. "There's a program that's similar to Habitat for Humanity that goes to Africa to help the smaller tribes and colonies. They need people to help with building structures for hospitals and schools. I thought about applying but didn't because of the responsibilities with magic and vampires."

"Psh!" I waved my hand through the air. "Don't worry about that. You should go for it! I've got the vampire side of things. So the next time you're at the campus, apply for the program."

She dug the toe of her shoe into the sand, looking down. "It's probably too late now..."

Rolling my eyes, I grabbed her shoulders, shaking her in a teasing manner. "Just do it, would you please!"

Laughing, she swatted me away. "Alright, alright. I'll apply. But I can't guarantee they'd want me."

"They'd be stupid not to want you."

***

"Are you sure you'll be alright?" Rhiannon asked, parking the car.

"Sitting in a car? Yeah, I think I can handle it," I said with sarcasm thick in my tone.

Rhi glanced at the clock, grabbing her bag. "I'll be back in about two hours, as soon as class lets out."

"Would you just go? You're going to be late." She frowned, so I added, "I'll probably just piddle around town a bit and circle back to the car. Or maybe call Wesley and talk with him for a bit."

"Just don't exhaust all your power. And don't let anyone see you talking to him. I can only imagine the questions they'd ask. And don't forget to lock the car if you leave. And—"

"Go to class!"

With one final look of hesitation, she reluctantly handed me her keys and left for class. I told her I wanted to ride along to get out of the house for a bit because I was bored. The truth? I was on a hunt.

This was the only way to ensure that neither my mother nor my sister would stop me. Rhi would be busy with class and Mom assumed I was with Rhi. It was a win-win.

I waited in the car for a bit before leaving. As I waited, I called Wesley, not the least bit fazed about using my power. Since the first few times I'd connected with Wesley, my power had grown. I learned how to use it without consuming it all. I used less and less of my power each time I called him. That, or I'd grown strong enough to not notice.

"Hey, Wes," I greeted, lounging in the passenger's seat which was reclined as far as it would go. "Long time no talk."

He chuckled, his laughter as smooth as the day in the bowling alley. "I know. A whole 23 hours. And still, I missed you."

Hearing those words warmed my heart because I knew he wasn't teasing when he said he missed me. He said it often—as if we were dating. And a part of me wondered if, in some twisted way, we were. Just because he was dead, and our only communication had been through a phone, it didn't diminish our feelings for one another. He was still the charming, cute guy I'd gone on a date with.

He'd told me once or twice that he would take me out again if he could. That he would choose somewhere more private, where we could spend time together without a bunch of other kids from school distracting us.

I'd dreamed of that date: sitting in the basement, snuggled up on the couch as we watched a movie. We'd share a bowl of buttered popcorn—because according to Wesley, it was a crime to eat popcorn without loads of butter. He'd slip his arm around me, coy but cool, and I'd rest my head on his shoulder, our hands brushing against one another's as we both grabbed popcorn at the same time.

That version of our date—the wholesome version—had filled my heart with glee. Yet, it also left me empty to know that it would never happen.

But it was the less wholesome version of that date, the one where Wesley would lean in and brush his lips against mine in a soft kiss, that had truly haunted me. Because I wanted it so desperately. And knowing that it was never within reach had made the heartache that much more apparent.

One of these days, Wesley. I'll help you like you've helped me. I'll save you.

"I missed you, too." My voice was soft, conflicted with what I wanted and what I had.

"I have information you might be interested in," Wesley said, his tone now serious.

Cocking an eyebrow, I said, "I'm intrigued. Do tell."

"Well, I was listening in on some other conversations, and I'm pretty sure one of the lieutenant vampires is going to be somewhere around the mall."

Based on our calculations and observations, there was a hierarchy to the vampire community. We believed that certain vampires were in charge of others. Danny and the other suspects, such as Clayton, were low on the totem pole—the "minimum wage" employees. Assuming Danny really was a vampire. That had yet to be proven, but the evidence highly suggested it.

"The mall is closing," I said, glancing at the clock. "I'll never make it there in time."

But did that stop me? Nope.

Wesley said they'd be on the Auntie Anne's side of the mall, telling me to be careful, a worrisome expression on his face. But before we hung up, he blew me a kiss.

That was a first. Was I supposed to catch it like they did in the movies? Blow him one back? This was new territory for me—for *us*. So, I smiled and told him I'd call him soon.

Locking up Rhi's car, I cut through one street, down another, crossing the town with all the shortcuts I'd mastered throughout the years. What would take others at least an hour to walk, only took me 15 minutes.

The mall was already dark when I got there. All the cars in the lot were gone, save for a few who were still locking up. The nearly empty lot had an ominous presence. So eerie. I was waiting for something to jump out and grab me, pulling me into the dark shadows.

There were no patrons walking around and no cars driving through the lot as they left the mall. I was alone. If someone wanted to hurt me, now would be the perfect time.

Instantly, I started to regret charging to the mall with such haste. Maybe I should have stuck around the campus, got a little more information from Wesley first. But stupid me, always ready to jump into the deep end without my floaties.

I turned the corner to the Auntie Anne's entrance. Dark. It was much darker than any other entrance I'd seen yet. *Too* dark.

That ominous feeling became so intense, it felt like that moment in the woods when I could feel the eyes of a monster watching me, but I couldn't see them. That's exactly what it felt like; that I wasn't alone. Whatever was here with me, it wanted me dead.

Nope. Uh-uh. I'm out.

I'd swiftly turned on my heels, noping myself the heck out of there, but was stopped by a familiar voice.

"Isabel Dufort. I thought you'd show up eventually."

Squinting my eyes in the dark, I muttered, "Coach Terry?"

I had a feeling he was involved with the vamps, but I didn't expect him to be here waiting for me. Frankly, I didn't think he had the intelligence to pull off setting a trap. But he'd been expecting me, which meant he knew that I was watching—and that Wesley was listening in. He knew.

That was what shocked me.

Without wasting any time, my magic lifted the enormous flowerpot beside the entrance pillars, slamming it against him. His body fell to the ground, ceramic shards clanking against the concrete. He groaned— enough of a sign to let me know he was alive. Enchanting the plant, leaves wrapped around him and enveloped his body.

While he was wrapped up like a burrito, I ran. If I wanted to fight, I needed to be in an area that was lit enough to see where was striking.

But he was too quick, breaking free of the leaves and grabbing my leg as I ran past him.

I hit the ground *hard*, the pavement scraping against my face, tearing through the fabric on my sleeves and knees. Standing over me, just enough of his face was illuminated for me to see the disgusting smile that had curled into his lips.

"I'm going to have so much fun with you," he cackled, taking slow, daunting steps toward me. "I'm going to sever your limbs from your body, feasting on your flesh while you still breathe. And when you think you can't handle anymore, I'll bring in your family so they can watch me bathing in your blood."

He licked his lips, salivating at the thought.

But I wasn't about to give up. I flipped onto my back, lifting my hands to guide the metal "pedestrian" sign that I'd ripped from the mulch with my magic. Hovering behind him, I held it there, waiting for the right moment to strike.

Sniffing the air, he sighed in pleasure. "I wonder what a young witch's blood tastes like?" he taunted.

With an edge to my tone, I said, "Too bad you'll never know." Then I smashed the sign into the back of his head.

Gripping his wound, he turned to see what had just hit him. Well, if he wanted to know, then I'd show him. Waving my hands back and forth, the sign slapped him repeatedly, one side of his face to the other, before I used as much force as I could muster to break the metal sign from its stand, ramming it through his abdomen.

Falling to his knees, he yanked the makeshift stake from his stomach, tossing it to the ground. His hands gripped at his abdomen, blood pooling at his knees.

I lifted the metal stand from the ground, aiming it for the back of his skull. Doing this hard enough to kill him would take a lot of power, so I took a deep breath to prepare myself.

About to deliver the final blow, my plans were thwarted by a massive gust of wind that rolled through, so precise, it was as if a mini tornado had been summoned just for our fight. An invisible force—which felt like that same daunting presence I'd felt in the woods, or in the parking lot earlier—lifted Coach Terry from the ground, carrying him away.

It rescued him! That must mean…

He wasn't the leader.

Coach Terry wasn't the head vampire. That force, that gust of wind— that unknown presence—was clearly the one in control. And it was stronger than I could've imagined.

Knowing that the presence was there, but not being able to see it, left an uneasiness in the pit of my stomach. It sent a shuddering wave of fear through my very core.

In a panic, I ran.

After the power I'd used to rip a sign from the concrete, break the metal in two, and beat the vampire with it, I was exhausted. My limbs were heavy, like I'd been carrying extra weight. Despite the exhaustion, the fear and adrenaline kept me alert and alive, pushing my feet forward with each step.

I had no idea who that presence was. But I did know one thing, *that* was our true enemy. The one who called the shots.

The one we needed to destroy.

Chapter 12:

Broken

The terror had hit me so hard, I ran all the way back to Rhiannon's car, not taking half the shortcuts because I was too afraid to cross anywhere covered in darkness.

By the time I reached her car, I shook too hard to get the keys in the hole. Once I finally managed to calm myself down, I could think logically. But my body was so heavy, so weak, I needed a power boost.

Doing the easiest thing I could think to do in the moment, I posted an embarrassing picture of me making a fish face to every social media account I had. My eyes were wide open, my mouth puckered up like a fish, with my cheeks sucked in. I looked absolutely hideous in that picture. But I couldn't forget the caption—*Plenty of fish in the sea, so who wants to get with me?*

Oh god, that was cringeworthy.

Maybe I didn't need to post to all of my accounts, but I'd panicked. The constant worry of whether that presence would show up again had plagued my thoughts.

Rhiannon came back shortly after, immediately sensing something was off. On the drive home, I explained what happened, accepting any criticism of my stupidity.

"Let's just get home and tell Mom about it. She might be able to help us figure something out."

I nodded in agreement, already feeling a little stronger from the humiliating comments that were rolling in online.

We pulled into the driveway and as soon as I stepped out of the car, I began calling for my mom. Walking up the porch steps, I noticed Biscuits wasn't waiting like he usually did. Whenever I came home, Biscuits would always be waiting on the front porch, as if he were the house's guardian, protecting us from intruders. I'd have to worry about him later.

"Mom!" I called out, receiving no response.

Rhiannon's eyebrows were pulled in, concerned with the lack of reaction from our mother hearing us screaming out her name.

But when I entered the house, the atmosphere felt dark and ominous, like the presence I'd faced at the mall.

Taking a slow, steady step through the doorway, I peered around, calling out once more.

The entire living room was a mess. Furniture was overturned, things thrown around everywhere, and deep gashes in the back of the couch. And Biscuits…

The poor black kitty was lying on the floor, surrounded by a small pool of blood, his body motionless. "Biscuits!" I cried out, rushing to his lifeless corpse.

Rhiannon covered her mouth in shock, her eyes blotted with tears. "Do you think they're still in the house?" she asked. And I knew she wasn't talking about Mom, but the person—or things—that did this.

I shrugged, too shaken to call out again in case there was someone there.

We stood in front of the dark hallway, squinting to see the other end, but too hesitant to actually walk down there. Looking back and forth between one another, I grabbed her hand, and together, we walked down the hall.

Even down the hall, everything was trashed. Bits of broken glass riddled the floor, no doubt from the various vases and flowerpots we had on display. The wall had deep scratches running along the length of the hallway, leading to our mother's room, the door ajar.

Rhi and I shared a look of trepidation as we pushed open the door, revealing... absolutely nothing. She wasn't in there.

"Where the hell is she?" I asked, growing in fear with every passing second. My heart pounded in my chest, pumping blood through my veins so fast that my hands were shaking.

"Unless she's in one of our rooms, I can only think of one last place to check," Rhi answered.

Still, we checked both of our rooms to make sure. Surprise, surprise, they were both empty.

We went down to the basement. The lights were off, leaving the room in darkness, except for the screen from the television that was lit up with the image of our house from the outside.

Halting our steps, neither of us moved, frozen in fear. I could understand now why that girl on the beach had simply stopped moving. The absolute terror and confusion had abruptly stopped everything—maybe even time itself. I couldn't even *breathe*, the fear ran through me so harshly, pricking at my nerves like little needles.

It was Rhi who took the first step, flipping on the light switch to see our mother lying on the floor.

Her chest didn't rise and fall with shallow breaths. Her limbs didn't twitch to alert us she was barely alive, barely breathing. She was still.

She was dead.

We didn't speak or move for seconds that felt like hours. It must have registered in Rhiannon's head first, as she was the one to spring toward our mother, diving to the floor to hold her body in her arms.

And that was when the anguish settled in. Rhiannon cried out in a loud scream, indecipherable and not holding words. Her cry was pure emotion, unable to form anything more than heartbreak.

But me? I couldn't move. I stood, rooted to my spot, unable to take in the sight before me.

A strange feeling claimed me, a pull that dragged me toward the window of the basement—the small window that looked out into the backyard. A dark figure stood at the edge of the woods, neither masculine nor feminine in its appearance. All I could see was a dark, humanoid form with two glowing red eyes watching me from within the trees.

I should have killed her when you were a baby.

Those words… They were a whisper through my mind, speaking to me from the presence outside. I wanted to turn around to ask Rhi if she'd heard it, but I already knew the answer. Those words were intended for my ears only.

Curiosity had taken over, pushing away the thoughts of my dead mother behind me. I had a new mission, one that I felt could solve what I refused to accept.

I tried to open the window, unsure what exactly I would accomplish in doing so, but it was locked. It wouldn't open, wouldn't budge. Cursing, I slammed my fist against it. Even my magic wouldn't pull it open.

The figure took a step back becoming enveloped by the trees and darkness, disappearing into a flash of smoke. And when he did, I heard a faint tune. The same tune I'd heard from my bedroom window that night Biscuits had alerted me that something was there.

Unable to do more at the window I forced myself to turn around, to face the truth.

My mother was gone.

Rhiannon sobbed, choking on her own phlegm as she clutched my mother's body in her arms. I crouched down beside her, placing a hand on my mother's arm. She was still warm, meaning it happened recently. After my fight in the parking lot.

When I'd felt the presence take the coach.

Oh, god! What if they did this out of revenge for me watching them, hunting them, fighting them? Was this my fault? Was I the reason she was dead?

"No," I cried out, begging it not to be true—any of it.

I stumbled back, staring at my mother from a distance. It was too real, too raw, to be so close to her while she was like that.

Walking over to the altar, I grabbed my phone from my pocket and placed it on the altar. Sitting on my knees in front of it, I closed my eyes and called out to our ancestors, just as my mother had done so many times before.

And so many times, I had teased her for performing her witchy stunts. *How stupid could I have been?*

"Ancestors," I said, my voice cracking in desperation, "please, come to me. Give me the strength to understand what happened. Help me to conquer the dark presence that plagues us. Please, allow me to speak with my mother."

Rhiannon's hand touched my shoulder, startling me. I looked up to see her eyes, puffy and red. But beneath the grief was a fierce determination. With a single nod of her head, she sat on her knees beside me, grabbing my hand for strength.

"Please," she called out, her voice raspy and thick. "We ask for your guidance." Her eyes were closed, so I closed mine again, focusing on our touch, our intentions, our pleas.

Something told me to open my eyes. I wasn't sure if the voice was my ancestors' or my own, but I opened them, nonetheless. The phone was lit up and my mother's face slowly growing clearer.

"Mom?" I whispered; Rhiannon looked up. Her hand squeezed mine, anticipation building, a blend of excitement, knowing we'd see her, and hesitation, knowing what she would be.

"Isabel and Rhiannon," she said, her tone soft. "My *daughters*." Her tone quickly shifted to spite. In a rage, her voice rose to levels I'd never heard, screaming how useless we were. "You simple-minded fools. How could you let me die? You're worthless—the both of you. I should have let that goddamned creature take you when it had the chance. You're both pathetic little bitches, unable to handle the simplest of tasks. I should have—"

"Be quiet, Mother," I cut her off and turned to Rhi. "Can you use that calming spell Mom uses for tea?"

Rhi nodded, doing as I asked, and we both faced my mother, waiting patiently as she yelled obscenities at us.

Her face had morphed from the angry lines drawn across her temples and the narrowed slits for eyes, into the calm expression we recognized.

"Mom?" Rhiannon asked, skeptical at first. But when our mother smiled and nodded, she knew that it was *our* mom and not the vile, angry creature that consumed her moments before.

For me, it was when she asked if we drank a cup of tea before the ritual. That was when I was convinced.

"I'm dead," she said, confirming what we already knew.

"Do you know who killed you?" Rhiannon asked, probably believing it to be the same dark presence I thought it was.

Mom nodded. "I have a history with that vampire. He's the reason for Isabel's scar," she said, motioning to my face.

Absently, I touched my scar, my frizzy hair flopping over my hand.

"I think it's time I tell you the truth about what happened that night." Mom took a deep breath, closing her eyes so tightly, it was as if the pain had stung her. When she opened her eyes, they were glossy, tears forming along the lids.

"You were a baby, Isabel, when that monster took you to his lair in the cave. I'd been neglecting my responsibilities as a witch and had let my guard down. Your father tried to warn me not to go in, but I was so desperate to get you back, I didn't listen. And when the creature overpowered me, it was your father who saved us.

"He cast a protection enchantment on the locket you wear so strong it took all of his life force, literally absorbing his physical form and soul right into the locket, which is why it is so powerful."

I clutched the locket around my neck. *He'd been there with me this whole time, and I'd never even known it.*

"When he did, the power was so strong, so immense, that the pure magical energy had burned into your skin, leaving that scar on your face. I'd used the rest of your father's power to trap the creature within the cave, though it was only temporary. He's back now, and he's more powerful than any other vampire I've encountered. Only the locket can protect you from that much darkness."

Rhiannon touched her fingertips to the phone, asking, "And it was that vampire who killed you? Do you remember what they looked like?"

"I know who they are, but not what they look like. Not exactly. You see, because I'm a witch, I can clear the fogginess that usually clouds a ghost's mind. I remember my death. However, I could not *see* the vampire who killed me. It was as if they were there, but they weren't. Nothing more than an invisible presence—an energy—blowing through the house like a tornado. Still, I know it was *him*. The same vampire from before."

Rhi and I shared a look of understanding, knowing that it was the same vampire I'd seen, too. Whatever his reason, he was back. And apparently, he was stronger than the rest.

"Even back then," my mother continued, "I couldn't get a good look at him. He was always shrouded in darkness—a figure made from the shadows themselves. But I have a suspicion that he is the one transforming and recruiting other vampires and has been for decades."

Rhi tilted her head slightly, interpreting our mother's words. "So, he's the top dog? The 'CEO' of the vampires," she quoted with her finger.

"In a manner of speaking, yes. We need to figure out who this vampire is. If we can find him and kill him, we can revert the other vampires back to their human form. Maybe even bring back those who they've killed with their fangs," she said, looking to me. "Though, that's a long shot."

I nodded, catching her intention. *If we can kill him, I might be able to bring Wesley back.* It may have been a slim chance, but it was there.

"But we must do it soon; before it's too late," she said. "Once they're fully transitioned, there's no going back. They'll have the power to turn others, and soon the whole town will be overrun with vampires—whether we kill the master or not."

The words sank in, sending a wave of nausea rolling through me. Cursing under my breath, I shook my head, trying to shake out the information for happier thoughts. Though, there was no ignoring it. I now knew that we were truly in deep sludge. And as if that wasn't bad enough, we were down our strongest soldier in the war against vampires. It was only me—the newbie—and Rhiannon—the girl who hated magic.

Great. Isn't that just freaking great! We were officially screwed.

"As I told you before, our family has kept the vampires at bay. But that bastard got me," she swore, taking me by surprise. For a second, I wondered if she'd reverted back to the angry ghost-mom. I wasn't used to her swearing. She must have been really shaken up.

Her eyes softened, her voice calm and motherly, like when she'd given me that pep talk before starting middle school. "I'm gone now. I'm not in your realm any longer; it's up to you girls to continue this journey on your own. But I will be here every step of the way to offer you guidance and support. All you need to do is call."

She smiled, warmth spreading through me, and I questioned whether that was her magic as a witch or her love as a mother that affected me so. Swiping a tear from my eye, I asked, "So, what should our next step be?"

"You need to place a magical barrier over the house. Rhiannon, do you remember how?" Rhi nodded, so Mom continued. "I'm sure the house looks like a fraternity party rolled through it," she said with a chuckle to lighten the mood, though neither of us offered more than a forced laugh.

"Don't worry about cleaning until you have your strength back. We'll need to disconnect soon so you can have enough power to create an impenetrable barrier. And don't forget to use our herbs in your tea. Drink it often. The magic infused within it will make you stronger as it goes back into your system. And because it was my magic infused in the herbs, it may be stronger and give you an additional boost. Take the wooden statue from the altar and place it by the front door. It can help serve as extra protection. That should be enough for now, until we speak again."

I glanced at Rhi, who bit her bottom lip to hold back the tears. Because we both knew it was time to hang up, yet neither of us was ready. Mom was our rock, our safety. Without her here, we felt powerless and vulnerable. Not to mention, the grief and guilt that tormented me from her death.

"Remember, you girls need to be strong, which means you need to stick together. Support one another. Don't let them tear you apart. He will try to divide you, single you out, and take you down like that. Don't let him. You are stronger than he is, but you need to work together."

Rhi and I nodded, grabbing the other's hand and holding it up, showing her our solidarity. She smiled in approval.

"I love you girls more than anything in the world—in any of the realms. Remember, I will be here for you anytime you need me."

We said goodbye to one another, promising to reach out to her soon. Then, Rhi showed me how to place a protective barrier over the house. Lifting Mom's body, we cleared the altar and laid her on top, using magic to preserve the body. Because the altar was a magical possession, we used it as a conduit to boost our own magic, making her preservation easier and less taxing on our powers.

I didn't realize it then, but my reluctance to bury my mother was an attempt to avoid the grief. I couldn't handle that she was gone and didn't want to believe it to be true, so I pushed back my grief, believing that I could figure something out—a way to bring my mother back—no matter how unbelievable it may have been.

We used our magic to fix the gashes in the walls and structural damage. But for cleaning the glass and broken items, we did that by hand, using good, old-fashioned elbow grease, so as not to exhaust our magic.

At this point, we were both on guard. Without having Mom—or even Biscuits—to help guard the house, we were at such a disadvantage. In fact, we were so disrupted and heartbroken by everything that had happened—and everything else to come—we slept in the same bed that night, both of us too afraid to leave the other's side for too long.

***

"Tink! Tink, come quick! Look!"

Rhi's shouts instantly put me in high-alert mode. Readying my hands for magic, I rushed up the stairs to her art studio, bursting through the door.

"What's wrong?" I asked, looking around frantically.

"You *have* to see this," she answered, waving me to come closer. She watched something on the floor.

I stepped closer, peering over her shoulder to see a life-size clay figurine of a person she'd made. "Oh, it's clay," I said, confusion in my tone. "It's... cool." I tried to feign enthusiasm, but I didn't see the big deal. She'd been practicing clay for a while now, and to be honest, this wasn't her best work.

"No, look," she insisted, pointing to it.

I squinted my eyes, unsure what I was supposed to look at, when I saw it. The clay moved in a slight, jerky motion.

"Did you see?" Rhi asked, her eyes wide and filled with excitement.

"Yeah."

"I wasn't enchanting it."

Now *that* surprised me. "It's moving on its own?"

"Isn't that crazy!"

The movements were awkward and short-lived, but there, nonetheless.

"It's like a new form of magic! Isn't that cool?"

"I thought you hated magic?" I asked, confused by her sudden happiness.

"Not when it's manipulative, like enchantment. But I'm not forcing this to move. It feels different. Like, I can feel my magic being used, but it's... I don't know... pure. It feels natural."

"Oh." That was all I could say. I didn't know how to react, or what that meant for us. It's not like a clay figure could help us defeat vampires, but it was cool. Whatever made Rhi happy. Though, I didn't understand how it was possible to move it without enchantment. That was something Mom might know.

Still, I plastered a smile on my face and said, "That's awesome, Rhi." I gave her the support she needed.

Chapter 13:

Stalemate

Training.

That was what my life consisted of, from morning to night. When I wasn't training mentally with my magic, I trained physically. Building my strength and agility, I worked out every day, no matter how much my muscles ached or my body cried out to rest. I pushed and pushed myself, much to Rhi's dismay.

"You need to rest," she pleaded, urging me to sit down and drink a cup of tea. But when I ignored her request, her voice turned stern, like our mother's, even calling me by my name and not Tink. "Isabel, sit!"

Rolling my eyes, I took a seat at the kitchen table. "You know, I'm not a dog," I groaned, rubbing my sore calves.

Rhi rolled her eyes in return, sliding me a cup of tea with Mom's *special* herbs—the ones she kept for only us and not the customers. The magic infused within those herbs was far stronger than anything we sold online.

Sitting across from me, she blew on her cup before taking a sip; the steam rolled around her face and disappeared into the air. "Speaking of a dog..." she said, placing the teacup on the table like Mom would. When she took on the role of caretaker after Mom's death, she also started behaving with some of the same traits. "There's a stray bulldog that's been lingering around the front porch, just like Biscuits did. Now, I know you don't believe in reincarnation, but it makes me wonder..." She chuckled, taking another sip of tea.

"I noticed him, too. He's always sitting there, as if he's guarding us. It's weird. Biscuits used to do the same thing. It's as if he replaced him. I may not believe in reincarnation, but I also didn't believe in magic."

Rhi nodded and I finally took a sip of my tea, allowing the herbs to soak in longer than Rhiannon. Peppermint, with a hint of lavender. And plenty of sweetener—just how I liked it. Within seconds, the calmness of the tea felt like a reset and my power levels returned to normal.

I wouldn't admit it, but she was right about resting. I felt loads better in a matter of minutes.

"So, what shall we call him?" Rhi asked. "And how do you know it's a him?"

I shrugged. "Dunno. I just feel like he is. We could always go out there and lift his leg," I teased. "It's strange… I feel a… familiarity with this dog. Like, I've met him before, though I'm not sure how."

"I don't know," Rhi answered. "But what I do know is that you can't keep skipping school to train. I understand that fighting the vampires is important, but you need a good education. Plus, the school will come knocking if you miss too much, and they'll want to speak to Mom. Do you want to explain she was killed by a vampire, or should I?"

Leaning back in my chair, I blew out a breath. "I know, I know. It's just… When I was fighting Coach Terry in that parking lot, he was so much stronger than me. Sure, I had my magic, but it took a lot out of me to do it. Without my magic, I was useless. A victim. I don't want to be in that position again."

"You can't take on everything alone, Tink. Remember what Mom said? We need to work together. Go to school and trust that I can be stronger than you think. Okay? No more skipping."

I nodded, silently stewing in annoyance. Yeah, she was right, but it still left me deflated.

After we finished our tea, she joined me in the basement, where I'd transformed the entire wall into a huge television screen. Rhi liked to tease me about it every time we were down here. And like clockwork…

"Just admit it, Tink. You want to watch Netflix on the big screen."

I rolled my eyes, forcing a dry laugh. "Har, har."

Plopping onto the couch, I whipped out my phone, pausing before I connected to Wesley. "Is that why you call me Tink? To tease me?"

Rhi nodded, a wide grin on her face. "Took you this long to figure it out?"

"I felt a small boost when you said it. Though now that I know the truth, will it have the same effect, since I won't be so annoyed when you say it?"

She shrugged, using her power to summon the TV screen to flip on. Though she didn't practice her magic like I did, she would help out when she could, like infusing the herbs, or using her magic for the TV while I used mine for Wesley.

Coach Terry appeared on screen at the same time Wesley appeared on the phone. "Movie time?" he asked with a knowing smirk, rolling his eyes dramatically as he said, "Oh, great. Coach Terry… again."

"Shut up," I teased with a giggle. "You know he's our best bet for figuring out who the leader is."

Wesley nodded, his face turning darker, more serious. "Just be careful. They know you're watching. I could hear him talking about it with someone. Not sure who, but he said 'the witch is watching.'"

Rhi and I shared a worried look.

"Well, we need to figure out who that vampire is, and this is our only option," I answered a little too defensively. To ease my tone, I teased, "I promise I'll be careful, Peacock Boy."

Wesley suppressed a grin. He wanted to smile, I could tell. But he was trying to assert the severity of the situation. "You better be careful. I worry about you, Is. If anything happened to you, I don't know what I'd do."

His eyebrows were creased, those blue eyes holding so much depth and compassion. Warmth filled my heart.

"Alright, lovebirds," Rhi said, pointing to the TV. "Let's save the romance for after our *movie*."

Wesley chuckled, his hand resting on his neck and a charming smile on his face.

We faced the TV—Wesley propped up on the pillow—and continued our daily afternoon activity: spying on Coach Terry. I'd been watching him like a hawk, even without Rhiannon's help.

But every time I thought I might find something, even a hint in the right direction, the screen would get cloudy, enveloped in black smoke. Yet, it only happened when the head vampire was there. Coach Terry was seen with clarity, but the master vamp? Those details were always blurred with smoke.

Hunting vampires had kept me busy—too busy to grieve my mother. I'd rectified the refusal to grieve by claiming it was because I was working so hard to bring her and Wesley back. And I was, though that wasn't the reason I had avoided my emotions.

I shook away the thoughts, refocusing on the screen. Again, pushing away the emotions with promises to deal with them later. One day. Just not today.

Coach Terry mentioned something about the ice cream shop at the edge of town. It was hard to follow only one side of the conversation. Whenever the master vampire spoke, it was filled with silence. Was he communicating through Terry's mind or blocking us from hearing his voice? And if he was trying to keep us from hearing his voice, was that because we would recognize it as someone we knew?

Wesley had heard his warning *the witch is watching*, which obviously meant us. So, why would he openly speak about a location? Was he trying to bait me, or was he oblivious?

So many questions that I didn't have answers to. At this point, there wasn't much I could add to the list of answers. Though the list of questions grew exponentially, turning into a web of uncertainty with too many connections that crossed but led nowhere.

The shadow disappeared from the screen, and I knew that meant the session was over. Might as well turn the movie off, if we were going with that analogy.

Releasing the connection, Rhiannon turned to face me. "Now what? It's surely a trap, right? If they know we're listening, then they wouldn't mention a location without expecting us to show." Her worried expression ate into me, feeding my nerves.

"Then let's give the vampires what they came to see. They want us to show? Fine. Let's do it. Maybe we can end them once and for all."

Was I scared? Absolutely. Did I mean everything I'd just said? Eh… I did and I didn't.

I wanted to show, but that would be going right into their hand, and who knew what tricks they would pull. How many vampires would be waiting for us?

"You can't be serious," Rhi said.

At the exact same moment, Wesley said, "You're out of your mind."

Basically, neither of them thought it was a good idea. And I agreed. It was a terrible idea. The worst. But there was one reason we had to do this.

"If we don't go, who will they kill? How many people will suffer if we don't take action? And not only that," I continued, listing out my concerns for discussion, "how many others will they turn? We can't handle them having a bigger army. We're already out of our league—especially with Mom gone."

"Still," Rhiannon protested. "I don't think it's a good idea. I say we wait this one out and see what happens. Maybe they're just trying to lure you in and have no intentions of hurting or changing anyone. Did you think of that?"

I turned to Wesley, already regretting asking for his opinion because he sided with Rhi.

"Why don't you hang back and let me spy on them some?" he offered, trying to find some middle ground.

"And if you see something, how do you expect to let me know? You can't call me, Wes. You know that."

"Then why don't you reach out to me every hour for an update," he suggested. "If I see anything suspicious, I'll let you know."

Reluctantly, I agreed. But did I listen? Of course not!

When the time came, I snuck away from the house, not even bothering to get the bike. I'd walk there. I knew enough shortcuts to get to the edge of town within an hour. As I crept away, the strange dog that had been guarding our house followed me through the woods, walking just a bit ahead of me the entire way—as if he knew where we were headed.

"You seem to know your way around," I said, feeling silly talking to a dog. But what felt even more ridiculous was that he looked back, as if confirming my statement. "You know, you seem so familiar. You remind me of our cat Biscuits. Though, he died recently."

The dog slowed its pace to walk beside me. Okay...

Still, I kept talking. Maybe it felt good to get it out, or I just needed someone to listen without thinking I was crazy or giving me a look of pity. But I spilled my guts to this interesting creature that seemed too wise for an animal.

"Mom died, too. Both by the same hands. It's why I'm going to find him. That vampire. I want to put an end to his misery, so no one else has to grieve."

The dog looked at me, his head cocked slightly.

"Alright, maybe a *sliver* of that is revenge. But do you blame me? He destroyed my father, killed my mother, my cat, my Wesley." Yes, I realized how stupid that sounded, saying *my* Wesley—but in a weird way, it felt true. Wesley really did feel like he was mine. Not in the sense that I owned him, but that I considered him my friend, my family, my... dare I say, boyfriend? Love interest? Crush? Whatever the word, he was it.

And it killed me to know that we could never be more because of some stupid vampire.

The dog stepped in front of me, stopping me in my tracks. He stared at me hard for a moment. I had no idea what he was trying to tell me—if he was trying to say anything at all. Maybe he was hungry and wanted a snack? I had no clue, but it helped to pretend.

"I know, I know. You're right. I shouldn't be going after the head vampire. Mom, Wesley, Biscuits—they're gone now. I know that! But it's too much for me to accept. Can't I just live the lie a little longer? Let me believe I can actually kill this guy and get them back?"

The dog turned swiftly, resuming our walk, though he stuck beside me.

I was only halfway to the edge of town when the atmosphere in the woods shifted. Silence fell over us. The dog stopped walking, his tail sticking straight out behind him, the hairs on his fur rising. Emitting a low growl, he slowly stepped in front of me.

The forest was dark from nightfall, but in an instant, it became pitch black, enveloped in darkness. And I knew... it was *him*.

This was it. This was what I came for.

Without wasting a second, I used a big portion of my magic to lean the treetops, allowing the moon to peer in through the opening. Casting that light on the darkness, it slowly morphed into a humanoid figure of shadows. Was he tangible? I hoped so.

Whipping out the knife I'd stowed in my pocket, I used my enchantment to make it soar through the air, striking him in the chest. My hands clutched the air in front of me, as if holding the handle, and I swiped them down. The knife sliced through his chest and abdomen, all the way down to his non-existent belly button. A dark mist poured out of him.

Just when I thought I was safe, the knife pulled out and flipped through the air—from the magic that wasn't mine—and came flying back at me. The dog leaped up, knocking me over right as the knife would have struck my neck.

I turned around, the knife was stuck in a tree. But when I turned back, he was gone, leaving a cloud of dark mist slowly evaporating.

Relief filled me until the disappointment settled in.

Once again, I lost him.

With my shoulders slumped in defeat, I thanked the dog for his help and yanked the knife from the tree. I walked forward, still heading toward the edge of town, when my feet tripped over a large lump.

No. Oh no. Please don't be...

It was a body.

Whipping out my phone, I turned on the flashlight, shining it over the body of a woman. I didn't know who, but I carefully examined her for bite marks—starting with her neck.

Nothing. Not one bite. No blood. No wounds. Her body was still warm, but she was pale, with a frightened expression on her face. As if she'd been literally *scared to death*.

I stepped back, realizing how badly I'd messed up. I'd touched the dead body. Were my fingerprints going to be on her now? Was that possible?

Glancing into the trees, I saw a pair of glowing red eyes, and a big, toothy smile, filled with taunting malice.

He wanted me to see.

I ran back home, bursting through the door and calling out for Rhi in a panic, quickly putting away the knife. There was no way I'd call the cops when I had a knife on me. Even without knife wounds on her, they'd assume I killed her.

Rhi was mad when I told her what happened, but she quickly forgave me, knowing that I was right about them killing someone.

"So, it was just him?" she asked, after we'd made some tea and brought Wesley into the conversation. "There weren't any other vampires"

I shook my head.

"I wonder why," Wesley said, his eyebrows tight in confusion and skepticism. "Do you think he was trying to make a point?"

"How do you mean?" Rhi asked, taking a sip of her calming chamomile tea.

"Well, he knew you were listening. And on your way to the location, he shows up, without reinforcement, leaving behind a dead body. To me, it sounds like he knew you were coming. Not only that, but *how* you were coming, which route you took… And he came to warn you not to mess with him. I mean, there just so happened to be a dead body on the exact path you took? He did it on purpose."

The more Wesley spoke, the more certain he'd become.

"And what was up with that body? Why weren't there any bite marks? Is he even a vampire?"

Something in my head clicked when she said that. "What if he isn't? That would explain how he can move in the shadows and wind. Or how he could kill someone without biting them or leaving any blood. I mean, any vampire would want that blood, right?"

"Unless they're killing for sport. Or, like Wesley said, as a warning," Rhi answered.

"But still, no wounds? How is that possible?" I shook my head, assuring myself that I was on the right path now. "Think about it. It all makes so much sense. The knife flew back to me, as if someone else had possessed it. This creature knows we're watching, but how? He's stronger than any vampire Mom had seen because he isn't a vampire."

"Then what is he?" Wesley asked.

"He's a witch. Er, warlock? He's got to be. How else can he manipulate magic?"

"I don't know… moving in the shadows? Sounds more like demon stuff to me," Wesley teased with a smirk.

Teasing or not, he could be right. Whether it was a warlock or a demon, or even just an entity of pure evil, one fact remained. We needed to stop him, pronto.

***

Every time I went after him—that magical, warlock, demon guy—it was the same result. I'd just missed him, but bodies were left behind. One at a time, of course, but they were always waiting with no bite marks, blood, or wounds. And every time, their faces are filled with terror, frozen in time until their bodies could decompose, allowing their face to finally be free from fear.

How messed up was that?

The more I chased him, the more I came up empty-handed. But I knew he couldn't evade me for too long. Eventually, we would meet, face-to-face, and I would end his reign of terror for good.

Chapter 14:

Vanished

It took a lot of practice, but I'd finally figured out how to have both Wesley and my mother present at the same time. I liked to call it a magical conference call.

Their faces were side by side on the screen, though there weren't defining blocks to separate them like there were on a typical video chat. Still, they could not touch one another. It was like they were together, but they weren't.

"I think I've almost found their meeting spot," Wesley said. "A place that holds AA meetings, and I'm pretty sure that's where they're getting their new recruits. It's like, some kind of initiation or something. I don't know, but it's definitely suspicious."

Mom nodded, tapping her finger to her chin in deep thought. "It makes sense. Vampires go after the weak-minded. The ones who desperately want something. Maybe they're unsatisfied with how their life turned out, or they crave wealth and power they don't have. Their desires hold them back and claim them. That's when he swoops in and offers them everything they could ever want. Eternal life. Power. Strength. He sells them a pretty package, and they eagerly agree, too consumed with greed to think against it."

An insightful interpretation, and realistic for sure.

"I'm not sure which location they're at," Wesley said. "It might not even be in town, but it's worth looking into."

And I planned on looking into it.

The following day, I asked the counselor at school for every AA meeting within a 50-mile radius. She probably thought I was crazy. I knew she thought I was an alcoholic because I overheard her gossiping in the teacher's lounge about me. She referred to me as *the weird girl with the alcohol problem*. I got a magical boost out of it, so all in all, it was a win.

Over the next week, Rhi and I drove out to each AA meeting, finding nothing more than alcoholics supporting one another through the struggle. It was an inspiration, really. I admired the way they listened to one another intently, applauding each person for sharing their truth.

That was why he recruited people from AA—he targeted people who were down on life and easy to recruit.

Our being there felt like an intrusion—given we weren't alcoholics—so we'd quickly slip out when we realized they weren't vampires, moving on to the next location.

I was on the verge of giving up, forcing myself to continue, though I was filled with dread every time.

Until one day, I heard it—that tune. The one that I'd heard from my window and the night Wesley drove me home and the night my mom died. I knew that we were in the right place.

"He knows what we look like," I said as we stood outside the entrance. "When we go in, we'll need to be quick. If he recognizes us, it's game over." I flung my hood over my head to look inconspicuous.

Rhi nodded, doing the same. "We don't need to go over the plan again. I got it."

Opening the door with as much discretion as possible, we slipped inside, locating the meeting. Peeking around the doorway, there was a room of people, some of whom we knew, looking at the man who stood at the podium—tall and slender, he stood with confidence. His skin was milky pale, dark hair swept back, revealing his handsome features that were almost statuesque.

But something about him was... off. Like a hologram, if you looked at him from the right angle, you could almost see the illusion. He had a quality about him that made him stand out as the leader—a confidence bordering on arrogance when speaking to the others.

Without wasting any more time, my eyes met Rhi's, and we both nodded. This was it. Time to teach that son-of-a-monster a lesson.

Raising my arms into the air, I did exactly as Mom told me to, manipulating the clock to stop time. Everyone in the room froze.

Everyone except for *him*.

With a wide, toothy grin that resembled the one I'd seen in the trees with the glowing red eyes, he took a step forward from the podium.

"At last," he said in a tone that was too cocky for my liking. "We meet."

Without hesitation, I raised the podium from its base, smashing it into him repeatedly until he dropped to the ground. I took several steps forward to see if any damage had been done—though, I kept my distance in case of any surprise attack.

Battered and bruised, he lay on the ground, not breathing. Was that because he wasn't human, or was he dead?

Suddenly, his eyes jolted open, his body swung upright, and he knocked the podium away from him. He rose to his feet and, with an evil glint in his eyes, he lunged forward to attack.

My locket glowed bright and seared his skin, melting it. In a flash, he appeared before me, as if untouched by the flames.

Again and again, I attacked him, only for him to avert my attack. Even when Rhiannon and I tried to double down on him, he was too quick. How was I supposed to kill someone who wouldn't die? Then again, he couldn't kill me either. Every time he tried, my locket would protect me. But how long would that last?

"We can exhaust ourselves fighting, or we can get to the bottom of this now," I said, holding up my hands in retreat, giving him the universal sign for a truce.

He chuckled, his laughter evil enough to pierce my flesh with goosebumps. "Speak for yourself," he said, stepping closer. "I can do this all night. I have an eternity."

I narrowed my eyes. "Then, let's go," I growled, holding out my locket.

With an amused expression, he threw up his hands in surrender, taking a step back. "I guess we are at a stalemate."

My hand gripped tight around the locket, not daring to let go or move my stance. "What do you want?" I asked, my tone filled with contempt. "Why are you here? In this town?"

That eerie chuckle returned. An uneasiness settled deep in my stomach when I gazed upon his expression. His tongue glided over his lips and a dark smile curled at the corners. "I'm hungry." His eyebrows rose suggestively, almost as if he were filled with lust from the thought. "I want blood."

It was lust, alright. *Bloodlust.*

My eyes narrowed to slits as disgust filled me. "Why us? You were here once before. Why did you come back?"

He sighed, like he was happy to answer. "Ah, a town of great treasure. Time is fickle, is it not?"

What the heck did that mean? Why was his answer so cryptic? I rolled my eyes. Why bother trying to decipher that? He'd probably intended for it to confuse and distract me. "Why does everything get cloudy when I watch you? I know you're the one doing it."

He met my accusation with a smile. "I'm the oldest."

"The oldest vampire?" I reiterated.

"I am." He nodded once. "I'm the oldest, so I can do as I please. Even if that means eating every human that crosses my path. If that is my prerogative, then so it be."

"Why?" I asked, lowering my hand only slightly as it was sore from being held up for so long. "Why do you want to kill all the humans?"

He frowned, shaking his head. "You misinterpret. Without humans, I would starve. That's why I recruit lieutenants to bring me food from all over the world. They satiate my hunger, my thirst, without eliminating an entire town."

"How can you feel no shame?" Rhiannon asked from behind me.

"Do you feel shame when you squash a bug? No, because you are the stronger being. But now *I* am the stronger being, and that terrifies you, little witch." He paced around me, my body slowly turning with every step. "Or, should I say, little *bug*?"

I refused to confirm what he'd said, regardless of how true his statement was. My heartbeat quickened, my blood pumping hard enough that he could no doubt sense it.

"I could eat animals," he said, his voice wistful as he pouted. "It's just so boring."

Rhi scoffed, her tone filled with sarcasm as she said, "Oh, *boo hoo.*"

He disappeared from in front of me, reappearing in front of her face. "Such bold talk for someone without a locket." His finger ran along the side of her cheek, his nail leaving a trail in its wake. "Especially for such a weak witch, so out of touch with your magic."

I struck him—not with my magic, but with my hand. I swatted his hand from Rhiannon. "You keep your disgusting fingers off my sister."

Tipping his head back, he laughed. "She doesn't need your protection. She has her own."

My eyes scanned her body, looking for any sign of a locket like mine, but she didn't have one. All she wore was a bracelet with a small charm shaped like a leaf. *The charm!* It was made from clay.

Was her protection coming from her clay? Or had Mom enchanted the clay before giving it to Rhiannon?

But the way he spoke, with such nonchalance… was he lying? Trying to lower our defenses and catch us off guard? I didn't know what to believe anymore. Apparently, neither did Rhi. Based on her look, she was just as lost.

I stared at the man who towered over us, shrouded in mystery. "What's your name?" I asked, but he simply turned and walked away, toward the podium, flicking the cap off a man who was frozen in place. He evaded me. *But, why?* "Why won't you tell me your name?"

Turning swiftly on his heels, he faced me. "You can call me the Elder, the Great One, the man with the devilishly gorgeous looks," he said with a wink, mocking me with every word. His arrogance was astounding.

"You know, I was once a curious human like yourself. Thirsting for knowledge, deeply craving satisfaction in a life so drab." His voice, his motions—they were so animated, like a performance. Perhaps, that was exactly what they were.

"However, I have found a new *thirst* for life. And you can, too. One taste of blood and you'll understand the euphoria. It's simply exquisite."

I couldn't tell if he was trying to convince me to join him, or desperately overselling his position as the master vampire. His behavior was too theatrical for me to believe his lies.

"Something tells me you're full of crap. Admit it, you're a warlock! You've figured out how to use magic to turn people, but you're not a vampire, are you?"

A clever smirk crept onto his face, and he shook his head. "Ah, the fool who believes they hold wisdom."

Mimicking his tone, I said, "Ah, the monster who evades all questions."

He chuckled as he neared. Even through his amused demeanor, I could see an edge of tension building. "Do not mistake my actions for evasion. If you want answers, little witch, I will give them to you. Starting with the reason I'm in this town. I want to feast on your human friends. I will do more than taste their blood, I will eat their flesh and their bones, if only for you to feel the guilt of knowing it was your fault. A pathetic child could never compare to my power and wealth."

"And yet, you can't kill me," I taunted, throwing it back in his face. "The 'powerful, wealthy' vampire," I quoted with my fingers, "can't defeat a pathetic child."

His lips curled into a smile, and he laughed. "Yes. Rather a nuisance, isn't it? Fear not, I have the means to end you. But I think I'll drag it out." He turned away, his laughter growing as he added, "I'll make you suffer before I tear you limb from limb."

I had no doubt he wanted to do the things he promised. But still, something wasn't adding up. There was something in his words that was a lie, I'd just yet to figure out what.

No more of him dominating the conversation. I planned to trick him into revealing his secrets. "And how would you kill me? Hm? Because I don't think you can." Maybe if I taunted him enough, he would start blabbing.

"There are many ways to kill your kind. Just ask your mother or father. Oops," he said, covering his mouth with a chortle. "You can't ask them. They're dead. I killed your father and your mother, and next, I will kill your sister."

"You're a liar!" I screamed, my voice echoing in the small room that stood still in time. "You didn't kill my father. He sacrificed himself to save me!"

"Yes," he hissed, appearing in front of me. "He sacrificed himself because of *me*. And so will everyone else you love, because that is what I do. I bring anguish to the world. I taunt you with regret until your mind goes mad. I am chaos, and greed, and lust, and pain, and torment."

While he rambled on with his nonsense, I discretely used magic to pull the wires from a computer on the table behind the stage. They slithered along the floor, jabbing him in the ankle. His body shook and vibrated, the electricity coursing through him before he fell limp.

Falling to the floor in a lump, he appeared dead. Yet, he stood back up, brushing himself off, a menacing scowl on his face.

"Mark my words, pathetic witch. I will kill every human on this planet in the most excruciating way."

I scoffed, not allowing his words to affect me. "Then how would you eat, genius?"

With a clever smirk, he redirected the conversation, once again. It was as if he was tormented by a life of death and killing, yet thrived on it all the same. He wanted his torment to be everyone else's.

I shared a look with Rhi, hoping that she would understand my expression, the message I tried to convey. If I could end the freezing spell, we could attack him at the same time, hitting him from both sides at once.

Nodding once, I ended the freezing spell, and we both dove for him together. Before we could wound him, he vanished, leaving us standing in the middle of an AA meeting for vampires.

Chapter 15:

Game

Time passed and the master vampire had essentially disappeared. Not once had he made his presence since our brawl at the AA meeting. We'd seen no activity from him—or any other vamps—and it left me both relieved and uneasy.

Everything was quiet, which was good. Right? I couldn't help but wonder if our talk had changed anything, though a part of me knew it couldn't be true. Not for a being as evil as him.

Maybe we scared him away? Or perhaps, he figured it wasn't worth the hassle and moved on to a different town. As desperately as I wanted to believe that he simply gave up, my gut insisted otherwise. I couldn't shake the foreboding feeling that this was nothing more than the calm before the storm. The big, nasty storm that would suck up the town in its drowning clutches.

As if the uncertainty about *why* he left wasn't enough, I also couldn't keep myself from speculating on *who* he was. His identity, despite his proclamation of being the head vampire, was still a mystery to me. Did I believe him?

If he was really as old and strong as he claimed, then surely, he could kill me in a fight. The only thing that stopped him was my locket, but was that really enough to make him end the war *just like that*?

The thought had passed my mind that he was possibly a low-standing recruit and he was afraid to battle us—though that thought quickly passed. He wasn't as weak as he tried to play off. He knew he was the only possibility of bringing my mother or Wesley back. That killing him was the only way to bring the other vampires back to their human form. And without him, I had no chance of doing either.

Maybe *that* was why he'd simply vanished into thin air—to wait it out. Until it was too late.

For the longest time, I'd wondered *why here?* Of all places, why come to a small town in the middle of nowhere? Surely, he would've blended in much better in the city. Maybe he got tired of this small town and left, like everyone believed Wesley had.

Speaking of which, even Wesley hadn't seen any traces of our vampire enemies. Mom was stumped, just as baffled as to why they disappeared. With no new information, and everything *eerily* peaceful, all I could do was prepare for when he came back.

Because something told me he would be.

Still, I hadn't given up watching our vamp-cam—as Wesley called it. And it was a good thing I didn't because they were planning something. A move was coming. A *big* one.

And it looked like it would happen at the big championship game.

***

Cheers echoed across the field, chanting and screaming erupting from the stands. The smell of hot dogs was enough to make me gag, but the buttery scene of the popcorn that wafted through the air reminded me of Wesley, shooting a pang of guilt through my chest.

"Should we split up?" I asked, looking around at the crowd of people waiting for the restroom. "We can cover more ground."

Rhi shook her head adamantly. "Remember what Mom said—we're stronger together. Plus, safety in numbers, right?"

I nodded, my eyes scanning over the hundreds of heads across the bleachers. "Where should we start?"

"Considering your visions are always in the locker room, I think we should start there."

Using my magic, I flipped the lock to the back entrance of the school, and we slipped inside, undetected. It was dark, except for the lights that scattered throughout the cafeteria and hallways, not lighting up the entirety of the school, but enough for our faces to be on camera if we walked too far.

Following the same thought pattern, Rhi pointed to one camera and the red light dimmed until it disappeared. Moving onto another, she took out each camera, masking our presence in any way she could.

We crept to the boy's locker room, where the home team—our team—would be. Standing just outside the door, we listened as Coach Terry gave the team a pep talk. Though, Rhi and I knew it was no ordinary pep talk that one would expect from a football coach.

"We're going to slaughter them tonight, boys. Every one of them. We will walk away victorious, proving ourselves once again."

The guys cheered—a ruckus of noise on the other side from them banging on lockers and patting one another in their pre-celebratory triumph.

"We will stain the field with their blood!" Coach cried out, his performance almost as theatrical as his master's. *I guess he learns from the best...*

Rhiannon and I slipped away to discuss our next move.

"What do we do?" she asked, her tone filled with worry. "We can't just barge in there and kill them all. They'd overpower us."

"Maybe not. We're stronger than you give us credit for," I reasoned, imagining the scene in my mind—Rhiannon and I charging into the men's locker room to burn them all to ashes. "But I don't think it's a good idea to go in yet. We need to wait for the right moment to attack. Besides, if someone caught us, what would we do? Declare they're all vampires? They already think we're crazy, then they'd think we're murderers, too."

Rhi nodded in agreement. "The best we could hope for was that they'd think we're perverts trying to peek in on the guys changing. The last thing we need is the sleazeballs in town to start hitting on us because they think we're easy. Trust me, you don't want those guys coming after you. They make vampires seem wholesome."

She laughed, though I could tell she was in no mood for jokes and was only trying to lighten the tension in the air.

"Let's head back to the bleachers for now," I said. "Maybe we'll see something there."

We crept back out of the school, walking around to the field to take a seat with the rest of the crowd. Climbing the bleachers, we settled into an empty spot in front of Rachel, Amanda, and Lindsay. I cast her a subtle smile, enough to let her know that she was still dear to me, even if things had been so crazy.

"What do you think, Tink?" Rhi asked, giving me a small boost of power where she could. "See anything remarkable yet?"

"I don't know, Egghead," I retorted, earning a frown. But hey, mocking was a two-way street, and she could use a little boost herself. "Looks normal to me."

Rachel laughed behind me, louder than necessary, which meant she was getting ready to roast me in any way possible. Though tonight, I was looking forward to it. I needed every bit of strength and reveled in the power.

"Hopefully I'll be able to see the game past all this frizzy hair in my way."

Amanda laughed, adding her own quip. "With obviously dry and split ends."

Rhi was less enthusiastic about the torment than I was, and she snapped, "Piss off!" She didn't even bother to turn around. Still, her words left the other girls speechless.

I chuckled, nudging her with my elbow. "What happened to the don't-let-them-bother-you attitude?"

"We have stuff to do, and their teasing is too distracting."

"Yeah, but they were giving me a boost," I answered with a shrug.

The entire town stood in the bleachers, cheering on the team. This was the big game, the championship, that everyone attended, whether you had a kid in school or not. Whispers passed through the stands, noting how amazing the team was this year—how they were so strong and fast.

Watching the field, I noticed that they *were* fast. Extremely fast. More so than they should be. They led the score with more than double the points of the other team.

"You should have seen the way Coach trained the guys," a townie beside me said to her friend. "I mean, it was rigorous, every day. They had a new schedule and diet. Apparently, it works."

Glancing over the field, I noticed the coach at the other end, looking at something. Or someone. "You got those binoculars?"

Rhi fished them from her purse, handing them over. I looked through them to see Coach Jordan, from the opposing team, nodding to Coach Terry. He smiled, flashing a fang, and I nearly dropped the binoculars.

"Look," I said, handing them over.

Rhi peered through, surely seeing the same thing I had because her face grew pale, and she looked at me in shock. "Both teams?" she asked. "Are they all vampires?"

I shrugged, not sure what to believe anymore. The plot had thickened, and I didn't have a spoon big or strong enough to stir it.

"What if the master is pitting them against one another for sport?" Rhi suggested with a shrug of her own. "Maybe they got bored playing against humans and wanted a challenge?"

"That's sick," I said, scrunching my face in disgust.

"That's vampires."

I laughed at the pure absurdity of it. Or maybe I laughed because despite how ridiculous it sounded, I could actually believe it.

Do vampires really care about sports? I thought all they cared about was blood.

During halftime, the teams headed back into the locker rooms as the cheerleaders and band put on a special performance.

Slipping back into the school around the back entrance, we headed to the locker rooms with as much discretion as possible.

"Should we watch them on the phone?" I whispered, holding out my phone in preparation.

"He knows when we do that," she answered. "I wish there was some other way to see them, without him knowing we're there."

I looked around my eyes catching on the vent above us. Point up, I asked, "What about the vent?"

She wasn't initially pleased with the suggestion, but with no other ideas coming to mind, she hoisted me up, insisting I go first since it was my idea.

Pressing my palm flat against the vent, I enchanted it to be silent as we crawled through. Once we reached the locker room, we peered through the slits to observe.

It was only the master vampire and two coaches in the room. Both coaches were big and muscular, like two bears. But the master was still taller than them both, and despite his slender appearance, he dominated the room.

"Terry, since you have obviously beaten Jordan in this game, you will be rewarded with a halftime feast," he said, his tone even but with devious intention.

Groaning, Coach Jordan said, "I've already spent so much time recruiting, initiating, and training my team. It's too much of a pain to train those jerks. Losing men won't help, either." Isa thought back to an early vision she had of cloaked figures standing in a circle like in a secret initiation ceremony.

Irritation filled the master, and he grabbed Jordan by the throat, raising him in the air as if he were lighter than a feather. "You dare tell me what to do?" His tone was laced with contempt and anger. "Your vampire brethren deserve to be rewarded with a feast, as per the agreement."

Coach Jordan raised his arms in surrender. "It's only halfway through the game. There's still time to turn the score around." He choked out, his voice quivering with panic through the strain of being suffocated.

Pulling Coach Jordan closer, the master tilted his head as he watched the man like a predator with its prey. "If you feel it is such a nuisance to train the new vampires, then let me make this easy for you."

In one swift motion, he ripped Jordan's head from his body, tossing it to the floor like a paper ball.

Rhi and I covered our mouths to muffle our gasps.

"There will be no weak men under my supervision. Here is your prize, Terry." He gestured to the headless body on the floor, blood pooling out around his black, leather shoes.

Filled with conceit, Terry dove in to *feast* on Jordan, declaring his team could have the scraps.

The master watched in disgust, clicking his tongue as he turned away, repulsed by the greed and utter lack of shame. Then, he walked away.

It was safe to assume that scene was over. Not wanting to spend a minute longer listening to Terry slurp up the blood, Rhiannon and I backed out of the vent, hopping to the ground again.

Knowing that Terry was alone and the master was distracted, we burst into the locker room with confidence that we could kill a low-level vamp such as himself. Without any hesitation, I pressed my locket to his skin, not giving him a chance to fight back before he burned to ashes.

In a way, I was burning, too—with rage. After seeing the way the vampires dismissed one another, without a care or concern… it was vile.

Glancing at the bloody mess around us, I asked, "What should we do with the mess?"

"Let the vampires handle it," Rhiannon answered in spite. "Since they're so good at cleaning up their messes." She turned on her heels, marching toward the door. "Besides, we have bigger fish to fry right now."

We left the locker room, heading back down the hall, toward the back entrance. That was when I felt it…

That ominous breeze had returned, alerting me we were no longer alone in the hallway. Appearing from nowhere, the master vampire stepped forward, only feet away from us.

Rhiannon got into stance, holding out her most powerful weapon. Her hands. Her *magic*.

With a shake of his head, he chuckled. "You think you can kill me? You're too weak!" Circling around us like a vulture, he added, "It would be a wasted effort, as I'm not the *master vampire* that you seek." Rounding back to our front, he stopped.

"If a fight is what you want, then I shall deliver."

He lunged forward, knocking me to the ground. The locket glowed and sizzled his skin.

Wincing, he jumped to his feet and backed up. Certainly not dead— barely even wounded, really—daggers filled his eyes as he stared.

He was pissed. No, he was absolutely *livid*.

"What's wrong? You mad that a big, bad vampire can't defeat a simple little teenager?" I taunted, my eyes narrowed and my face like stone.

His eyes drifted from me to Rhiannon, and before I could react, he pounced, throwing her across the room like a ragdoll.

My hands flew through the air, trapping him in place as I helped my sister to her feet. "It won't hold long," I muttered, walking her out until she could get her legs working again.

We escaped the locker room but now what? How we were supposed to kill something so powerful—in front of a football field of people, no less?

Stumbling along the hallway, we ran into Rachel and her trio, knocking some of their stuff to the ground in our haste.

"Hey!" Rachel snapped, grabbing her phone from the floor. "Watch where you're going, freak!"

"We need to get out of here!" I shouted, grabbing her by the wrist to pull her along.

She jerked her arm from my grasp and sneered. "Yeah, right. Like I'd go anywhere with you."

Lindsay stepped forward, her eyes filled with concern. "What's going on?"

"I know it sounds crazy, but the team is made up of vampires and they're killing people around town. Now, we need to get out of here before the head vamp comes back."

Amanda scoffed, rolling her eyes. "How stupid do you think we are?"

"Yeah," Rachel agreed. "I think we'd know if our boyfriends were vampires."

But Lindsay didn't budge. Her eyes bounced back and forth between me and her friends, uncertain who to believe.

Turning to her, I blocked the others out, focusing only on her face. "Lindsay, you have to believe me. I'm telling you the truth. Please, I know we've lost touch recently, but I swear I wouldn't do anything to hurt you. We need to leave. Now."

Rhiannon nodded in my peripheral, adding, "She's telling the truth."

Maybe it was the pure expression of fear and terror or the panic in our words, but Lindsay took a deep breath and nodded. "What do we do?"

Her question caught me off guard. "Do? Like, help?" I asked, sounding stupid as I pieced words together like a caveman.

"Our power grows stronger through torment and teasing," Rhi answered, her words rushed to accommodate the situation.

"Powers?" Rachel asked from behind Lindsay. "Okay, now I *know* you're screwing with me."

Before I could explain, the master vampire flew into the hallway, a massive gust of wind following his presence.

"Girls, grab your phones," I shouted to be heard over the loud whistle of the wind. "We're going viral."

If anyone could boost my powers, it'd be the queen of teasing.

Catching on, they each whipped out their phones, hitting record as Rachel poured her Slushie over me on the live feed, the smell of blue raspberry and cherry invading my nostrils. I'd be lying if I said I didn't sneak a taste.

"Hope this cools your burn, bitch!" Rachel shouted, throwing the cup at me. But behind her actions was something I'd never seen: a glint in her eyes, a beam of pride—not for herself, but for *me*. Like she was doing it to help and not tease.

Following her steps, Amanda dumped her Diet Coke over me. The carbonation stung my eyes, but it was worth the pain for the power.

And power, I had.

Thanks to their live feed, my power increased so rapidly, I could feel it pumping through me like blood through my veins—a blend of feelings pouring into me at once. It stung, yet soothed. Ached, yet pleased. It was both a blessing and a curse, a burden and a relief.

"That's enough," I said, throwing out my hand to the girls. "Now, get out of here before you get hurt."

They looked at one another with hesitation, slowly putting their phones into their pockets and backing away. Though, Lindsay was the most reluctant, as she didn't want to leave me with a beast.

I forced a calming smile and told her, "Go."

She nodded once, disappearing around the corner with the others.

"It's just us now, monster. Let's end this war for good."

Chapter 16:

Denial

The power thrummed through my body, lighting up every nerve in a fiery intensity that surged through my limbs, to my fingertips.

I'd never felt power like this. It was almost too much to handle. But my mother's face popped into my mind, calming me as if she were there with me. Her smile appeared, letting me know that we could do this. Together, Rhiannon and I would finally defeat the monster that stood before us.

Moving into the stance I'd practiced at home—one that was supposed to assert dominance and prevent me from being knocked down easily—I readied my hands.

"You really wish to fight me, *little bug*?" His maniacal laughter only fueled me, his words enhancing my magic. Did he not realize his taunting had given me power?

I shook my head. "No. I'm going to *end* you." My tone was filled with determination, sending a shiver of anticipation through me, because I knew that this fight would be the last. Only one of us would walk away and I would make damn sure it was me.

He cackled, amusement in his expression. "We'll see about that."

The lights in the hallway burst, one by one, until the only light that shone was where we stood, highlighting our battle in the spotlight. Though, no audience was around to see it.

I whipped my hand to the side, jerking the vending machine from its position in the corner, smacking into the side of him. But unlike Terry, he wasn't fazed. The machine flew across the hallway, crashing into the wall. Pieces of plaster crumbled to the floor, the white dust settling over the massive dent and laminate flooring.

But I didn't slow down long enough to wait for him to move. I pulled out the chair at a random desk and broke it from the metal base, using a piece of the metal as a spear. Piercing it through his chest, he slowed but didn't stop.

His fingers gripped around the metal, yanking it from his body, black smoke oozing from the wound. With a growl, he chucked the piece back at me, missing but almost hitting Rhi. The metal rose from the floor and flew through the air again, headed straight for my sister's heart.

"No!" I lunged forward, tackling her to the floor. But then the piece flew again, and I was the target. Inches from piercing my skull, Rhiannon stopped the metal spear, grabbing it with her hand after her magic gained control.

"I'll watch your back," she said, helping me to my feet as she stood. "You be offense, I'll be defense."

I nodded and looked back to our enemy who had disappeared. Where was he? Looking around, I didn't see anything but the destruction of the school hallway. Eh, I wasn't crazy about that hall, anyway.

"Where are you?" I called out as my irritation grew with every passing second. "Come out and face me, coward!"

A cackle sounded from above and around, in every direction, the sound getting louder. "Foolish children."

Materializing before me, his hand struck me across the face, sending me back several feet, crashing into a locker. My body hit the floor, unable to move.

"Tink!" Rhi shouted, running to my aid.

Every classroom door was wide open, books and desks flying out of each room and down the hall, aiming for us. With one hand, she helped me up again. With the other, she ripped the front off a locker and used it as a shield for the books that came flying at us, beating them away the best she could.

"We're gonna need more than a locker," I said, grabbing her hand and running down the opposite end of the hall. My feet stumbled, a shooting pain running through my leg from how I'd landed. Rhi's grip on my arm tightened, helping me along as I pushed past the pain.

She dove into a classroom, yanking me inside. I hobbled to the desk and Rhiannon grabbed her charm, holding it to my leg. A soothing motion swept through my calf, a minty tingle, and my leg instantly felt better.

"Thanks," I muttered, standing up. "We can't run forever. We need to strike him before he corners us in here."

Rhi nodded. "It's risky, but what else do we have to lose?"

Ducking out of the classroom, we nodded to one another before heading down the hall. Books riddled the hallway; desks were flipped in every direction. It looked like a tornado swept through and left nothing but destruction in its wake.

But what was eerie was the silence. Outside, cheers could be heard from the game, the announcer calling out different plays. But inside, there was no sound besides our footsteps on the squeaky laminate floor.

With hesitation, I turned the first corner and peeked before I walked out but saw no sign of anyone. *Where was he?* I continued down the hall with slow steps, ready for attack.

A crash from behind stopped us in our tracks. It was the hallway we'd just come from. Turning on my heels, I sprinted back in that direction, where I saw him.

Wind swept through the hall into a cyclone that surrounded him as he hovered in the air. I gathered as much of my power as I could without using it all and manipulated the wind that he produced, pulling the cyclone tighter against him until he was suffocating within his own power.

My magical grip on his tornado tightened, squeezing him within the grasp of his wind as I held him in place. But my power was dwindling, and I hadn't struck yet. Not really. I'd only held him in place, my fear prolonging the inevitable—that I'd have to release him and fight.

"Keep him like that a bit longer," Rhi said. "I have an idea." Snatching up the metal from earlier, she held it steady before him, aiming for his throat.

"I can't hold on much longer," I warned; Rhiannon nodded in response.

Just as she readied to strike, the cyclone swelled, bursting with a force that sent us flying into the lockers.

Grabbing my side, I winced, easing myself to my feet. Rhiannon lay crumpled on the floor, struggling to raise a shaky hand.

I got to my feet, rushing to Rhi, but I didn't have time to reach her before I felt the wind pressing against my back like a palm, knocking me down to my knees.

Pulling the fronts off the lockers, I created a barrier for us as we regained some energy for the fight. The wind whipped at my back, the force too powerful for me to do more than crawl. Each whip stung, but I couldn't stop, couldn't slow down.

Rhi unsteadily rose to her feet, giving me a single nod of assurance that she was ready. We were both battered and bruised, but not giving up. Together, we lunged forward. Knowing from our last encounter how quick he was, Rhi enchanted all the posters that lined the hallway, wrapping them around him in a paper cocoon. Knowing it wasn't enough, fabric from the home ec room flew down the hall to add another layer, until he was swaddled like an evil, immortal baby.

I walked up to him and held out my locket, ready to burn him now that he couldn't move. But as I neared him, something was off. It was his expression—it was too… calm. He was about to die and his lips were curled into a smirk? It was too calculated an expression, causing me to falter in my steps.

Just as I reached him, he burst free from the wrap, pieces of fabric and paper flying in every direction, sending me back a few feet. I glanced at Rhiannon, who was frozen in place, unable to move, her eyes wide in terror.

"Give up, witch!" His voice echoed through the hall like a boom, uncorrupted by the wind. "You'll never defeat me. I have more power than you could ever hold." Using that power, he pushed me down to my hands from a distance, taking slow steps closer to me.

"Tink!" Rhiannon screamed, her arms still plastered to her side from the force of his power.

My head was pressed against the cold floor between my palms, kneeling before him as if in worship.

"Bow to me," he said. "Pledge me your allegiance, and I *may* let you live."

There was a taunting in his tone—an amusement as he kept us frozen, his little puppets on a string, moving at his whim.

Everything I'd done had been for nothing. The training, the magic—it didn't matter. In the end, he would win because he was older and stronger. I was stupid for believing a teenager could defeat an ageless, immortal being.

Images of my mother passed through my mind. Never again would I tell her I loved her. Never would I be given a chance to thank her for being such a great mom. He'd stripped me of that right. Just like he'd stripped Wesley of the right to grow up and graduate from this town to do something with his life—possibly with me.

He'd taken so much from so many people. All the lives he'd claimed and the vampires he'd turned… he ruined their lives for his own sick game.

My body burned and seethed with rage, knowing that once again, he would be free to reign in terror as he pleased, with no one to stop him.

But the tremendous force holding me down was too much.

"Bow!" he demanded, shoving against me with the force of the wind.

"I… will… *never* bow… to you," I grunted, my voice strained.

His arms rose in the air for his final strike. "Then you will die!"

Rhiannon screamed my name and as she did, a figure smashed through the wall. The distraction was enough for me to regain the use of my limbs. And when I turned my head, my mouth gaped open in shock.

Rhi's life-size clay figure had come to life. The movements were still jerky and awkward, but it stood and walked on its own.

The clay-man took heavy steps toward the monster, who was too stunned to react. Or maybe the magic from the clay had somehow stunted his ability to move. Grabbing his arms, the clay figure held the monster in place.

I walked forward and pressed my locket to his forehead.

His skin sizzled from the touch, but he couldn't get away this time. I grabbed his arm, my grip burning his skin. The scent of burned flesh stung my nostrils. The deep, sickening smell of death lingered in the air.

"Fuck!" he screamed, trying to pull away, to disappear, but he couldn't. I was too strong now, filled with the magic of my ancestors, lending me their power to bring balance back to our world.

"You're not getting away this time," I growled, my skin so hot, I could feel the fiery heat radiating from my skin, hotter and more blinding than even the locket. "I won't allow you to kill anyone else. *Ever.*" I pressed the locket against him harder, searing every bit of flesh that remained.

His body burst into a massive flame, the wind around me still blowing with incredible force, threatening to spread the fire. But my fire was contained, only focused on him. Despite the flames that had enveloped us both, I couldn't feel the stinging sensation, so I pushed harder and harder, until he disintegrated into the same pile of dust the others had befallen.

And with that, the wind died down, blowing away his ashes as it settled.

Limping to my sister, I collapsed on the floor beside her. Exhaustion caught up with me and my eyes fluttered closed, the blurry image of the hallway the last thing I saw.

Chapter 17:

Vulnerable

Voices surrounded me, bringing me back.

"I can't believe she's a total badass! I know this might kill some of her power, but that was so cool."

It was... Rachel? *Was she talking about me?*

"It's alright. I'm sure the threat is over for now."

Was that Rhi? Talking to Rachel? Where was I?

"Are you going to take her to the hospital?" Lindsay asked. As she did, I felt a hand on my head, moving in a soothing, circular motion.

"Nah. I can heal her at home. But I'm sure she'd like the company after she comes to," Rhi answered, no doubt smiling. I could hear it in her voice. The relief and happiness—the ability to finally stop and breathe.

My eyes slowly opened to see Rhiannon sitting in the front seat of her car, Lindsay and Rachel at my side in the backseat.

"She's awake!" Rachel said with far more enthusiasm than I expected.

From the passenger seat, Amanda droned "woo-hoo" in a dry tone.

Lindsay grinned, her eyes dotted with tears. "I'm glad you're okay. I was so worried."

"What you did back there," Rachel said, her voice softer than I'd ever heard, "it was amazing. You saved us."

Though she hadn't exactly apologized for her bullying, it was implied. And that was enough for me.

"Thanks."

We stared at one another for a moment, so many questions unanswered.

"Alright girls, I should probably get her home to rest," Rhi said.

Before Rachel closed the door, I asked if she could set up a social media account to have a constant supply of teasing to keep my power boosted to protect the town. Sure, we defeated the big, bad vamp, but who knew what else was waiting for us?

On the ride home, I asked what happened back there after he turned to dust. Rhi had enough power left to repair the hallways and return the books and desks to the classrooms. The girls showed up and helped her, also carrying me out to the car.

"I'm proud of you, Isa." She glanced at me briefly before looking back to the road, a smile of pride beaming from her. "And Mom would be, too."

When we got home, Mom was the first one we contacted. Being passed out had given me enough strength to connect with her—though, Rhiannon helped—and she was ecstatic to hear what happened.

"I knew you girls could do it! You hold the same passion and strength as your father."

Looking away, tears blotted my eyes, threatening to spill over. "I just wish you were here," I said, my voice broken and raspy. Was it exhaustion or emotion that caused that? I didn't know...

"Don't cry, baby. You should be celebrating. What you did was incredible!"

"Yeah, but I thought it would bring you back! But you're not back. You're still... in here." I tapped the phone with my finger for emphasis. All I could do was talk to her. I couldn't feel the warmth of her embrace or the comfort of her touch.

All the grief I'd pushed away had finally surfaced. I sobbed into my knees, my body curled up to hold myself. Now that I'd defeated him and my mother was still dead, the reality had settled in that she would never come back.

"It was mere speculation, a hunch that was wrong. But it's fine, baby. You defeated the most powerful vampire, and that's what counts."

"But why can't I bring you back!" I cried, choking as snot poured down my nose, blending in with the salty tears.

Rhi extended an arm of comfort, but I pushed her away. I wanted to suffer and grieve alone.

"It's not fair!" I screamed, pulling at my hair in frustration. If Wesley could pull through the phone to strangle me, why couldn't I do the same?

And a thought struck me in that moment. *Wesley was filled with rage when he tried to do that, consumed by his emotions. What would happen if...*

Snatching the phone from Rhi's hand, I shoved my hand at the screen—no, *through* the screen.

Intensely cold air struck my hand, chilling me to the core. But amidst the freezing cold, I could feel my mother's warmth, her presence. Missing a few times, I'd finally got a good grip on her. Despite the mist, she was tangible enough to grab.

Using everything in me, I yanked her through, pulling my mother back into her human form. Her body slowly emerged from the phone as a mist, flowing through the air and onto her body, settling into place.

Then, there was silence. Nothing.

Until her eyes began to flicker, her chest slowly rising and falling.

Rhi gasped, her mouth gaping in shock. "How?" Her voice was breathless and filled with uncertainty.

"I don't know," I admitted. "But I'm glad Mom is back."

Wrapping our arms around her, we pulled her into a giant hug between the three of us.

I couldn't believe it actually worked. Maybe my emotions were so high, it allowed me to pull her back? Would something like that work on my father? Mom didn't think it would, so I tried. And unsurprisingly, it didn't work. I couldn't get a connection with him. The screen remained bank.

Moving onto the next attempt, I called Wesley.

"We did it!" I shouted as he appeared on the screen.

Wesley pumped his arm through the air, freezing when he noticed our little addition. His head cocked to the side. "Is that your mom?"

I laughed. "You're quite the sharp tool, Peacock Boy."

He rolled his eyes, a big grin plastered on his face. "How is that possible?"

"I'm not sure, honestly." I shrugged, laughing with a smile. "I thought of you and how you were able to reach through before you changed. And somehow, it just worked."

Wesley stared in awe, noting how amazing I was. I graciously accepted, my cheeks blushing with my mother's presence in the room as Wesley said something like that.

"So, are you ready to return to the realm of the living?" I asked, clapping my hands together. "We can figure out your story for your parents later."

Wesley's expression, a mix of sadness and guilt, sent an apprehensive wave of emotion rolling through me. Because I knew… he wasn't coming back.

"I'm not ready yet. There're a few things I'm still trying to figure out from this side. And until I do, I'd like to stay."

In silence, I nodded. Though, I couldn't help the disappointment that clouded me. We finally had a chance to be together. I'd been so excited about the possibility of feeling his touch, his embrace, his *kiss*—I'd never even considered that he wouldn't want to come back.

But it was his choice, so who was I to deny him that right? He'd already had it stripped away when he was murdered.

Still, it couldn't end like this.

Reaching through the phone like I had with my mother, I pulled Wesley out, just enough for the mist of his head and shoulders to appear. Half expecting him to be nothing more than vapor, I grabbed his head—which was tangible enough to get a firm grip—and pulled his lips to mine.

A shiver ran through my body from the cold brush of his lips. Yet, despite his frosty touch, a heat ignited through me, wishing for more; for the touch of his hands on my shoulders, pulling me into his embrace, for the affection that could have been so much more than a charming smile or a sweet laugh.

But this was enough. For now, it was more than I could've asked for. My first kiss was with someone I truly cared for, and even though he was a ghost with a touch that chilled my body to the core, it was enough to satiate my questions of "what if."

He pulled away slowly, resting his head on mine before I released him back to his ghostly realm.

Assuring me he'd have my back on the spiritual side and keep looking out for any other trouble in town, we disconnected. Wesley insisted I rest, and we could talk later. I agreed, though a part of me wondered what else he would want to learn from that side.

At his mention of resting, I realized how exhausted I still was. Fighting the vampire, bringing back my mother, connecting with Wesley… it came at a price.

My mother's smile was the last thing I remember seeing before everything faded to black.

***

"Oh, you're up?" Mom sat at the edge of my bed, holding out a mug of tea. "I had a feeling you'd wake up soon." With a wink, she added, "Mother's intuition."

Rubbing my head, I asked, "What happened?" I grabbed the mug, warm in my hands, and took a slow sip. Everything felt normal again. Yet, it wasn't. Then again, where was the line between normal and supernatural anymore?

"You used so much of your power in such a short period of time, you passed out for a few days." Her answer was so casual, so nonchalant. As if she were talking about the weather.

"I *what?*"

"Don't worry. Rhi and I managed to rewire a few memories from the students who witnessed everything. Nice girls, though that blonde one could do without the scowl."

I almost laughed at that statement. Never had I imagined Rachel being in the same sentence as *nice*, but experience had proven that anything is possible.

"Amanda's always like that," I answered, taking another sip.

"Unfortunately, they won't remember what you did, so they will probably retain their previous image of you."

I shrugged, unconcerned with such trivial matters. "Oh, well. They were never too fond of me, anyway." Besides, I figured things would return to their previous ways. Always destined to be the outcast—though now, the thought didn't leave me with a distaste in my mouth. Instead, it gave me strength, knowing that I didn't need their approval to feel good about myself. I'd defeated the master freaking vampire! You couldn't get much cooler than that.

"Except the girl with red hair like yours, only a bit more tamed, seemed concerned with your well-being even after we erased her memory."

Lindsay. I smiled at the thought, knowing Lindsay was as genuine as I always thought her to be. "Yeah, Lindsay is a nice girl."

"So, what happened with the vampires?"

"Those who weren't killed were changed back to their human selves, their memories lost. Though, that may be for the best."

She looked like she had more to say, so I shot her a look that said *get on with it.*

With a sigh, she said, "I don't think you defeated a vampire. While I was still dead, I saw him when he passed over. He wasn't human. Not even in a previous life. His spirit was filled with a mix of monsters. The most terrifying monsters I'd ever seen. More than just vampires."

And just like that, she'd confirmed my biggest fear—that we weren't safe. The master was gone, but more monsters lurked in the shadows.

"I believe we have only seen a fraction of the dangers that await us."

She stared at me for a moment, her eyes tipping back into her head as she began to sway.

"Mom?" I asked, jumping from the bed to catch her as she nearly fainted. "Mom!"

Rhiannon burst into my room, springing into action. She helped me lift my mother to my bed, brushing her hair from her face. "She's been having hot flashes since she got back. I think she's having trouble adjusting to this realm."

"Makes sense. I felt the other side and it was ice cold. The kind of cold that chilled me to the bone."

Rhi nodded, sitting at the edge of the bed with me. "Yeah. She said her body is still trying to adjust to the correct temperature." Lowering her voice, she added, "Though I think it could be menopause."

"I heard that," Mom grumbled, slowly sitting up. "Don't fuss over me, girls. I'll be fine. It just takes a bit. Remember, I was dead. What we've done... it isn't a part of the natural path of life."

A pang of guilt rolled through me. "Do you think we'll be punished by the universe for changing that path?"

"Only time will tell. Though intentions were pure, so I'd like to think not."

It didn't matter to me. I'd gotten my family back, and I knew they'd have my back, no matter what happened.

Stepping outside for some fresh air, I sat on the porch steps, looking out at the garden. The dog that had recently taken residence had emerged from the tree line of the woods, padding toward the house.

With a smile, I called him closer. But as he walked toward me, his body shifted into something else—something human. A slim man with blond hair that fell over his glasses.

"It's... *you*," I said in absolute disbelief. "James."

In that instant, I remembered exactly who he was—the kid in school who always seemed to blend in, to the point I forgot about his entire existence. The same guy I saw in the woods that night I killed the vampire with Rhi.

And here he was, shifted from dog to human before my eyes. Well, not human because he was obviously something supernatural if he could shift.

"Hello, Isabel."

He stopped a few feet away, standing in front of me with a soft smile on his face. Not knowing what else to say, I gestured to the porch steps. "Want to sit?"

Graciously, he took a seat beside me. "I'm quite impressed with how you defeated Pazuzu. I've never seen a witch with such a natural ability to innovate and enchant."

My head cocked to the side. "Pazuzu? The vampire?"

"That creature is no vampire. And yet, you defeated him with such talent and skill."

My mind swarmed with questions. "I'm sorry—who *are* you?"

He chuckled. "I'm the one who granted your family the power of enchantment."

"So, you're a dog?"

"And a cat," he added with a smile.

"Biscuits?"

He nodded.

"But I thought Biscuits was dead." This was all too weird, too crazy, even for me.

"That body is dead now, yes. But it was only a shell. I have the ability to morph into other animals. It makes it easier to keep watch over you and your family. I'm sure you wouldn't want some guy walking around outside of your house all the time." He let out a hearty laugh.

"Why do you watch us?"

"For security. You keep the town safe, but who ensures your safety? But, we can talk more about that later. We have much to discuss."

***

"So, you're not a wizard?" I asked, unsure if wizard was even the correct terminology.

James shook his head. "Nope, I'm an alchemist who's been around for a *very* long time. I've seen generations of your family use their powers."

"The powers you gifted us?" Because, according to James, he's the original creator of the enchantment magic my family held. I still hadn't wrapped my head around the fact that he wasn't just a quiet boy from class.

"Correct," he answered. "Your enchantment magic is rooted in alchemy. Just as alchemy can manipulate matter, your magic can manipulate objects. You see, I can use alchemy to change the properties in your windows. The pane is tough and sturdy, but I can make it malleable. I can make the glass bend. And so can you."

My eyes shot from the windows to his. "What?" I asked, still comprehending his words. We shared a similar magic? But he wasn't a magician or wizard, so how was it possible for us both to have similar magic? How was it possible that our magic was born from his alchemic manipulation?

As if sensing my doubt and confusion, he said, "Try it," his hand gesturing to the windows. "Make the glass bend."

I walked up to the window and placed my palm on the glass. "What do I do?"

"The same thing you did with the phone or the erasers."

My cheeks flushed at the thought that he'd seen me practice my powers by watching the erasers dance. I closed my eyes, focusing on the window. The glass was cool beneath my touch, shaded by the trees and the roof of the porch. I imagined the glass melting beneath my touch, becoming absolutely bendable to my will. My fingertips tingled and a sense of energy ran through my palms.

I opened my eyes to see the glass slowly warping beneath my hand. Like ripples in the water, the warping expanded beyond my fingers, to the edges of the panes. My jaw dropped and I faced James.

"Oh, my god! Did you see that? Isn't that wild?"

James smiled, his reaction cool and controlled compared to my excited outburst. "I see. You are gifted, Isabel, much more than any other witch I've seen at your age. No other fifteen year old in your family has excelled as you have."

I beamed, filled with more happiness than I could contain. His praise brought me so much comfort and confidence. Though I wasn't sure why, I wanted to please him, to make him proud.

"Isabel," he said, placing his hand on the glass beside mine. The energy that flowed in and around my hand had amplified, and the glass returned to its former appearance. "I'd like to teach you," he said. "To show you more of what your powers hold. You have great abilities. I want to help you control and mold your powers. To show you what you're truly capable of."

"That..." I said, pausing to consider what he was saying. He wanted to show me how to improve my powers. He was the very reason for my family's powers. Perhaps, he could be the one to change the source of our magic. Maybe, just maybe, he could make our magic less isolating and emotionally painful.

"That would be like a dream come true," I said, hoping I hadn't laid it on too thick.

He chuckled, tipping his head back as he laughed, his blond hair brushing away from his face. "I doubt you'll be saying that after a few hours of training."

"I welcome the challenge," I said. "But I do have a few questions about my powers."

"Your questions will be answered with time," he said.

Chapter 18:

Calm

Time had passed.

Everything in town had gone back to normal. Once again, we were the weirdo family on the edge of town. Yet, I felt good about it. Sure, I still wanted to belong, but it didn't bother me that I didn't. I think, more than anything, I just missed my friendship with Lindsay. I missed being able to go out and have fun without worrying about vampires or trying to fit in. I missed having someone to talk with, outside of my family and our witchy world.

But every now and again, when Rachel would tease me, I could almost see a glimmer of something more, a recognition of what I did, even though she had no recollection of it. Maybe, even though the memory had been erased, it still remained, buried deep within her somewhere.

Could magic really manipulate something as precious as one's memory? I didn't know. Even when I thought we could manipulate time, it was skewed. Nothing could be guaranteed. And things didn't always go as planned.

I still used the TV to spy on the town, looking for any hint of another monster like him, just waiting to strike. Though I didn't see anything out of the ordinary, I couldn't help but worry.

The thoughts played havoc on my mind, and every so often, I'd head to Rhi's studio to sit with her, if only to feel a little at ease.

She'd spent a ton of time in her studio when she wasn't in class or helping Mom with the business. Outside of her responsibilities, she worked nonstop on crafting other clay figures, even smaller ones, bringing them to life.

Somehow, Rhiannon had created her own form of magic, through the very creation of her sculptures, which got me thinking. If she could change the form of magic, was it possible to change the way we grew stronger? When I'd mentioned it to Mom before, she'd shut the idea down. However, now I had James to discuss it with.

Since he revealed himself, he'd been coming around the house in both canine and human form. Mom liked that James had so much ancient knowledge about magic—though I think that she was relieved to have someone so powerful hanging around to keep us safe. Rhi, on the other hand, was a bit more skeptical of James. *Why now? Why did he suddenly reveal himself?* But even she grew to like him.

When I mentioned to James about changing the source of our magic, he said, "When it comes to alchemy, transformation is always possible, given the right circumstances and a catalyst for change. However, if you want to change what fuels your magic, you must remember that it will fundamentally change your level of power, which must be grown."

That had become my new goal—finding a way to have magic without mockery and taunting.

Rhi and I were hanging out in her studio. I was discussing potential alternatives to gain power while she sculpted away, crafting amazing work with her hands. But when she ran out of a certain color dye for the clay, she said it was time for a trip to the store.

We headed downstairs to check on Mom. Once again, she was in her bra and underwear, rubbing a piece of ice over her head.

"I'm so hot," she said, nearly out of breath. "I don't know how to handle it."

I looked to Rhi, whose eyebrows rose in worry. "Maybe we can try to connect with the ancestors and ask them for guidance?" It was a suggestion, but I was coming up short on ideas.

Going to the altar in the basement, we lit the candles and chanted, performing our ritual the old-fashioned way that Mom always did. I asked them for guidance to help my mother, who was one of their own. "Please," I begged. "Show us the path."

An image appeared in the mirror, slowly coming into clarity. The black smoke from the monster clouded the glass. *Just like with the TV.*

Only, this time, the smoke had begun to clear. Behind the smoke was something much more horrific.

Snarling, terrifying creatures stood just outside the town's edge. I leaned in and squinted, trying to make out the details of the image, but the glass cleared, leaving only my reflection.

"Okay, you guys saw that, right?"

Epilogue

In the darkness of the night, a creepy tune played. A familiar tune, appearing only in the presence of evil. Some might believe the tune itself held malevolence and destruction. An ominous warning of what was to come. Others would believe it was nothing more than a tune. For how could a simple song hold so much intention?

In a pile of ashes lay a phone. The screen blinked rapidly as the ringtone echoed through the night in a wicked chant.

Conference call with Master and 664 others. Join call?

And as that haunting tune played, a father—trapped in a hell of his own—couldn't give his daughters the warning they desperately needed. They could no longer hear the tune because they were no longer looking. The eyes that once haunted them had ceased; the evil grin had vanished.

Despite how unrelenting his attempts, he couldn't reach them, couldn't warn them. It was impossible. There was no way for them to know. No way for them to be saved.

But with life came death.

And with death came a new beginning.